THE SEARCH FOR GABRIELLA

by

John Problem

(Copyright)

Index:

Prologue.

London. Ben's Inheritance.

Edward's Notes. Part 1.

Screenplay: Venice 1470.

Edward's Notes. Part 2.

The Gallery in Albemarle Street.

Edward's Notes. Part 3.

Cheapside, London 1590.

Edward's Notes. Part 4.

Gin Lane, London 1720.

Edward's Notes. Part 5.

Screenplay: The March to Magdala.

Edward's Final Note.

The Trip to Liberech.

Epilogue.

Prologue.

If you're sitting in the Bennelong restaurant at the Sydney Opera House, that is, if you're sitting in the big semi-circular window, then you have an all-embracing view of the harbour and the bay with Sydney's skyscrapers (none of them overly tall) in the background. If you fancy eating the chef's signature dishes, then you order his raw yellowfish tuna in a basil and mustard soy seed sauce vinaigrette, followed by blue-eye trevalla roasted on an etuve of baby summer vegetables (trevalla is a butterfish from the Antarctic). Chilled sake is a good accompaniment. You finish up with Valrhona chocolate cream. This is chocolate ice cream and gelato mixed with praline ice cream and caramelised candied pecans, and is much admired.

The young couple sitting at Table 5 have ordered these dishes, although the girl had been tempted to have the vanilla bean crème brulee with green apple sorbet. Maybe next time. Their heads are close together when they are not eating and they smile at each other a lot, although they seem a little sad. From time to time he places his hand on hers.

"So when do you have to leave?" he is asking.

"Term starts again on the 16th. So I must

leave next weekend," she replies. "And you? When do you go back?"

"I'm almost finished here now so I can go pretty soon. I wish neither of us had to go."

"Yes," she says. "So do I. But you will come to Prague soon, won't you?"

"Of course I will. As soon as I can. As soon as I get the go-ahead from my client. Maybe I'll be there for your concert!"

'Yes. Please try.'

The young man looks quite well in his dark suit. He has an amiable face and a confident manner. But the girl, she is a beauty. Truly lovely. Auburn hair piled high on her head, a slender neck with tendrils curling onto it, a heart shaped face, dark eyes under arching brows, a mouth which almost pouts, a feminine and gentle manner....

The young man's mobile buzzes. He groans. "Excuse me," he says, raising his eyes to heaven, and looks at the screen. It is a text message.

'Ur Uncle Edward seriously ill. Pls call asap.' and it gives a London number.

"I have to make a call," he says. "It's urgent. Won't be long, I promise." He strides off to the foyer. A waiter appears and clears the dishes, smiling at her. When he has gone she puts her elbow on the table, rests her chin in her hand, and looks out at the bay.

In a corner of the foyer, the young man calls the London number. It is his uncle's solicitor. His uncle wants to see the young man as soon as possible. He is very ill.

He walks slowly back to the table and the girl. He knows he has to go to see his uncle, without delay. They were very close. But it is difficult to leave her, the girl sitting looking pensively at the bay. She is so beautiful, he thinks, still marveling that she should be with him.

"Oh," she says. "I am sorry. For you and for me..."

He takes a long look at her as though trying to record every detail of her face.

"I'll come to Prague as soon as I can."

London. Ben's Inheritance.

I had to fly via Hong Kong and Bahrein so it took about 24 hours to get back to London, and I was too late. I sat by his bed in the hospital but he did not wake from his coma. He looked just like he always looked - a little pale, strong features and longish grey hair.   A fine-looking man. I felt very distressed and sat there and thought about how we had become really good friends over the years, even though we didn't see each other very often because of my travelling abroad with my job. We usually met up about twice a year, for lunch, near his art gallery.

His life had been interesting and varied. He had studied languages at the Sorbonne and taken a job as a travel representative in half a dozen different countries. Eventually, he gave that up and settled down near Oxford and became an antiques and bric-a-brac dealer. Then, after a few years - and to everyone's surprise - he had started an art gallery. In Albemarle Street in the West End of London, no less.   'The Edward Fletcher Gallery.'   He also gave up his usual dress style of sweater and corduroys for tailored suits and brogue shoes.

"When in Rome, or Albemarle Street,' he had said to justify this unusual display of self-awareness.

I had expressed amazement at the suddenness of this move from bric-a-brac to art, from dusty shop to glossy gallery. He confided to me that this was possible because he had come across some paintings by Italian renaissance artists and had found clients for them.
"They were what I would call secondary renaissance painters and it took me a while to place them with the right clients. People who were interested in art but didn't have the funds for the best. I had to find people who were happy with a good work by a painter out of a top workshop. And that's what I did, and the pictures were worth quite a bit."

He was full of interesting tales, amiable, and pleasant to everyone he met. In the art trade he was, not surprisingly, considered a bit of a parvenu. He had never married, although he had introduced me to a number of charming girls and glamorous women over the years.

I went to see the solicitor who gave me a copy of my uncle's will. He had left me his art gallery.
 "There are a number of files which he

prepared for you to help you understand the business," advised the solicitor. "The accounts are handled by a firm nearby. Your uncle seems to have assumed you would want to keep the gallery going. Rather than sell it off."

I told him that I would most certainly want to keep it going if I could.

"Are there any staff?" I asked him.

"There were a number of young women who managed the gallery when needed. Then there is a Mr. Dobri Denn who is a picture restorer. And a fellow called Boulton who is a runner. A finder. Goes about looking for pictures. Spends a lot of time in Eastern Europe."

He opened a drawer and took out a box file. "Your uncle left this for you. He didn't tell me what it contains. Except to say it's nothing to do with the running of the gallery." He passed it over the desk. It was an ordinary black and grey box file. On the front was written 'Gabriella da Gonzaga.'

"A particular girlfriend?" I asked.
"I think not," he replied. "If it were, he might have left something for her. Apart from gifts for Mr. Denn and Mr. Boulton, you are the sole beneficiary. The gallery is temporarily closed

pending your decision as to its future," he continued. He told me about my uncle's illness and death.

Finally he said, "Here are some notes your uncle left you on the running of the gallery. And these are the phone numbers of the people I mentioned. I know Mr. Denn is keen to speak to you soon."

I thanked the solicitor and left. Outside, I called Dobri Denn who suggested we meet for a drink up the road from the gallery, in the Rivoli Bar at the Ritz.

"Tackiest bar in town," he said. "But it's convenient and it was Edward's favourite."

It was indeed the tackiest bar in town and still is; gilt everywhere, gilded alcoves with scalloped ceilings, plus back-lit naked nymphs, leopard-skin covered bucket seats, huge ugly onyx vases, plastic chandeliers, art deco bar-stools. The only people there when I arrived were the barman polishing glasses and a man sat in an alcove, who jumped up and stuck out his hand.

"Mr. Fletcher? How glad I am to see you. I am Dobri Denn. Please call me Dobri." And he motioned me to sit. Dobri Denn had a broad, honest face, bright blue eyes and a muscular build.

"I am very sorry about your uncle. Edward was a fine man and a good friend. So may I suggest we drink to him? And may I suggest the cocktail named in honour of the painter, Giovanni Bellini. Edward's favourite painter. And Edward's favourite drink," said Dobri.

"I'm pleased to meet you, Dobri. You knew my uncle very well, I imagine," I responded.

"Yes. We worked together for many years. He was such a nice person. My wife said that if she hadn't married me, she might well have married Edward!"

"I wish I had spent more time with him. He was always such good company. But we never had time enough, I guess". I didn't want to become sentimental so I changed the subject and asked, "What's the art market like these days. In general, I mean."

"Focused on the modern, mainly. The mega-rich Russians and the Chinese and the top bankers, most all of them now want bright, modern stuff. Even Agnews has decided to concentrate on contemporary works."

"Agnews? Even them?"

"Too right. Founded in 1808. Broke in 2008. Sold off their building in Old Bond Street. Moved just up the road from us in Albemarle Street   Where they offer only contemporary stuff. I think it's a sign of the times. No large-scale old master gallery is viable anymore because there's a dearth of traditional paintings to sell. But that won't bother us."

"How do you mean?"

"Well, although your uncle's specialisation was indeed the old masters, his business was different from the usual. Edward specialised in the less famous painters of the Italian Renaissance. In particular, what you might call the second division Venetians.   The less well-known artists, students of the big names, workers in their workshops, copyists."

"Is there a good market for that?"

"Edward made it work. He had a gift for finding the right clients."

"And who are they?"

"Edward always said, 'Lesser masters are for the lesser rich. Not the billionaires, but the millionaires.'"

"And that's a good market?"

"The number of global millionaires grew 17% last year. How they measure it, I don't know, but it's an impressive figure. The rich can't hang stocks and shares on a wall to show their friends. So they buy pictures. Have you been to the gallery, yet?"

"Not yet."

"Well, you'll see that it's very well appointed and you'll see the client purchase book. Of course, we're not Colnaghi's, but nonetheless, Edward was quite successful."

"Where did he source the paintings?"

"Eastern Europe, mostly. Budapest and stations east. I went on a couple of buying trips with Edward, but Boulton is the real finder. I do the restoration work. And help with the attribution research. In the West, virtually every piece of art is documented. But in Eastern Europe not so much. And less so for the secondary old masters. We have to do a lot of research to authenticate and attribute paintings from over there. Boulton will tell you how he goes about finding the pictures."

I suggested we meet at the gallery in the morning and we parted.

Edward's Notes. Part 1.

Dear Ben,

I'm writing this on the assumption that you will be reading it after I'm gone. If you want to keep the gallery going, I've left you a file describing how I ran it and the important roles played by Dobri and Boulton. If you don't want to keep it going yourself, then I recommend you talk to them about what to do.

What I really hope you will do is read the rest of this file and take up where I left off with what I call 'the Gabriella search'. I was so close. It would be good if you were able to succeed in it for me, finally. It has become a bit of a personal obsession I suppose, but nevertheless I greatly enjoyed doing it. Please read these notes and see what you think.

But first, a technical matter. I am dictating this to my computer. Speech recognition. It took an age to train the software to recognise *my voice and style but we finally got there. So, if you come across any typos or weird spellings or odd phrases, you'll know why.*

The reason I'm dictating this is because I no longer have the use of my muscles. Shortly after we last had lunch I was diagnosed as having a motor neuron disease. A nasty one called amyotrophic lateral sclerosis which wastes all your muscles and leaves you paralysed. The mind continues working fine, but the body packs up. Totally. If you're lucky, it does it quickly; if not, it can take two years. In my case, it's happening very fast, thank God. The vocal muscle is the last to go. Anyway, enough of that.

The Gabriella search is about a portrait which I believe was painted by Giovanni Bellini in Renaissance Venice and which subsequently disappeared from view. Bellini was a top Venetian painter who flourished from 1450 to the early 1500s. I'm a great admirer of Bellini - he's a marvellous painter. And I was intrigued when I came across some references to this portrait which, to my certain knowledge, is not to be seen in any gallery.

I've been tracking it through wills, inventories

and diaries for quite a while and I think I may now be getting close. The portrait is of a young woman, Gabriella da Gonzaga. She was the daughter of a successful mercenary working for Venice. Was the portrait commissioned? Was Bellini painting her as the model for a Madonna or a saint in one of his religious paintings? I have no idea. I don't know the circumstances. But the portrait is recorded in the daily ledger of his workshop, which I was able to consult in the City Archives of Venice.

The curious thing is that there is no price against it. Also in the ledger, it's recorded that he signed it with a Z instead of one of the usual variations of his full name. But what does that signify? We do know that in the Venetian dialect Giovanni was called 'Zianbellin'. Why was it painted and for whom? I don't know. The only thing I'm sure of is that it was painted by him in his workshop, in 1470

VENICE, 1470.

FADE IN:

A small military camp sits in a valley. The sun shines on flags and banners fluttering from poles and tents. Horses are tethered in rows. Soldiers, dressed in multi-coloured uniforms, are occupied at various duties.

There are none of the normal shouts and commands; none of the usual banter. The men move about quietly, unsmiling, occasionally looking up from their work at a large bannered tent in the centre of the camp. They are concerned, anxious.

EXT. OUTSIDE THE TENT - DAY

An elderly DOCTOR, wearing a dark cloak and a mask with long projecting nose, comes out of the tent.

TANCRED steps forward. He is 25, athletic build, a look of competence and resourcefulness

> TANCRED
> What is your opinion, doctor?

> DOCTOR
> It is not the plague.

He removes mask and shakes herbs and spices from the nose.

> TANCRED
> But how is my father? Will he recover?

> DOCTOR
> I cannot say. Your father has a virus in the chest. He is very ill.... .

> TANCRED
> Can you help him? Can you make him well?

                    DOCTOR
          I have given him a medicine.

Tancred looks at him, then moves toward the
tent.

INT. THE TENT - DAY

On a truckle bed lies TANCRED'S FATHER. His
face bears the signs of authority and bravery
He is extremely pale, coughing frequently.

His arms and armour are heaped in a corner.

Tancred enters and kneels by the bed, his face
apprehensive.

                    TANCRED
          Father. How goes it?

                    FATHER
          I have something to ask you,
          Tancred.

                    TANCRED
          Anything, father.

                    FATHER
          It is about your mother. I want
          you to go and find her grave.

TANCRED
You never told me there was a
grave! Or where.

FATHER
In the town of Montebello. Find
out how she was. Put flowers on
her grave. You will do this,
Tancred? I did not honour your
mother enough. She tired of camp
life...and one day she just
left.... I should have
followed..... But there was
always too much to do.

TANCRED
Of course I will do it. But. We
could have done this earlier,
together. We shall do it now!
When you are recovered.

FATHER
Maybe...... Listen carefully,
Tancred You can do other things
I wanted to do. And failed at.

TANCRED
Failed at? You are one of the
best condottiere in Italy! How
can that be?

FATHER

It was because I fought for
different city states that I
failed.

TANCRED

Failed to do what, father?

FATHER

To get land for ourselves. To
have a place. A castle.... a
home. I failed to do this because
I did not fight for one city
alone. I changed too often. This
is not the way. One should
remain loyal to one master and
then he will reward you. Now it
is too late for me. You must do
it, Tancred.

TANCRED

A home? The camp is our home.

FATHER

It is not enough. You need to
have a castle and land of your
own. For you. And for your family.
This is most important. You must
have a place. A place where you
are master.

TANCRED
A man can be master in the camp.

FATHER
It is not enough. You will see.
Where is Siegfried?

SIEGFRIED (O.S.)
Here, Chief. I am here.

He enters immediately. Swiss, 6'6", a powerful
veteran of many campaigns.

FATHER
Ah, Siegfried. You know the
signs, eh? I don't have much
more time.

SIEGFRIED
(tears on his face)
Don't say that, Chief.

FATHER
Siegfried, old friend..... Will
they follow him?

SIEGFRIED
He is your son. He is capable.
And resourceful.

FATHER
Good.
        (he coughs)
Damnation, I regret going so soon.

SIEGFRIED
        (taking his hand)
Nothing to regret, Chief. We had
many good times.

FATHER
        (looking up at him)
Aye, so we did. So we did... I
must talk more with Tancred.

TANCRED
Father. Will you take some wine?

FATHER
No, son. Listen. I want to give
you some advice. Three things.
Firstly. Put not your trust in
Princes. Or Dukes. They are
unreliable. It would be best to
work only for Venice. Work well
for Venice and she will reward
you. Go and see the Doge. He is
a good man. But never under-
estimate him. Here is our contract
with him.

From under the bed he pulls out a leather satchel.

                    FATHER
          Take this to Venice. See the
          Doge and renew the arrangement.
          And build up the troop, get more
          men and horses. Ask him.

                    TANCRED
          Yes, father.

                    FATHER
          Secondly. Beware of Carlo Gonzaga.
          He wants to be Captain General
          for Venice and will do anything
          to get his way. Beware of him.
          And thirdly...

A paroxysm of coughing leaves him gasping for air.

                    TANCRED
          Father! Holy Mother of God!
          Father!

His father's coughing worsens and then suddenly stops. His head falls back. Tancred kneels by the bed.

EXT. OUTSIDE THE WALLS OF MONTEBELLO - DAY

A small, walled town sits on a low hill, by a river, fields spreading out beyond.

Tancred rides up to an arched entrance, where two GUARDS watch his approach.

> FIRST GUARD
> Welcome to Montebello. What is your business here, Captain?

> TANCRED
> I have come to see the Mayor on a private matter.

> FIRST GUARD
> What is your name, please?

> TANCRED
> Tancred Sinasilo.

A quick look passes between the guards.

> FIRST GUARD
> Tancred Sinasilo?

> TANCRED
> Yes. Kindly conduct me to the

Mayor.

> FIRST GUARD
> Certainly, Captain. This way.

INT. THE MAYOR'S OFFICE - DAY

Stone walls, a shelf of books by a desk, vaulted
ceiling. A shiny brass telescope on a tripod
stands at the window.

A knock at the door and the First Guard enters.

> FIRST GUARD
> There is a soldier outside who
> wants to see you, sir. He says
> his name is Tancred Sinasilo.

> MAYOR
> Tancred Sinasilo! Then we'd
> better see him. Let him come in.

Tancred enters.

> MAYOR
> Welcome to Montebello. What can
> I do for you,Captain?

> TANCRED
> I have come to find the grave of
> my mother and pay my respects.

MAYOR
And your mother's name?

TANCRED
Elisabetta Sinasilo.

MAYOR
Yes. Elisabetta Sinasilo. The
priest can certainly show you the
grave.

TANCRED
Good.

MAYOR
This may seem a strange question
but do you have any proof of who
you say you are?

TANCRED
Proof? To visit my mother's
grave! What nonsense is this?

MAYOR
Keep calm, Captain. I ask because
there is another matter.
Concerning your mother....
concerning la Donna Sinasilo. It
requires that, whoever says he is

Tancred Sinasilo, can prove it.
Of course, you can visit the
grave, but this other matter is
more complicated.

                    TANCRED
I have no proof of my name. You
can see I am a soldier. I have
no home except the camp. Where
everybody knows who I am.

                    MAYOR
Is your father alive?

                    TANCRED
No.

                    MAYOR
Ah. I am sorry. Let me call the
priest, so you may see the grave.
Then we will talk some more.

EXT. THE CEMETERY - A FEW MINUTES LATER

Tancred kneels before a headstone bearing his
mother's name. There are tears on his face.

INT. THE MAYOR'S OFFICE - SAME TIME

The Mayor looks through his telescope. He

sees Tancred at the headstone. He nods his head, seems reassured.

EXT. THE CEMETERY - SAME TIME

Tancred stands up, wipes his face with his sleeve. He looks at the countryside around and at the town.

INT. THE MAYOR'S OFFICE - A FEW MINUTES LATER

Tancred and the Mayor sit at a table with wine.

> MAYOR
> Captain, I wish to tell you about
> my problem. When La Donna
> Sinasilo came here many years ago,
> she found employment with a
> merchant in the town. He was very
> pleased with your mother's work -
> she did his accounts, helped him
> with his transactions and kept
> his business in good order. He
> prospered. He would have married
> her.... When he died he left
> half of his estate for a small
> hospital to be built in the town.
> And the other half he left to
> your mother, so that she would be
> comfortable for the rest of her life.

TANCRED
Was she happy?

MAYOR
Yes, she seemed happy. Ah, she
was a fine woman.....I admired
her exceedingly. However. To
come to my problem. When Donna
Sinasilo - I will call her your
mother - died, she left a chest
containing some money and jewels.
Her instructions to me were that
the chest was to be given to her
son Tancred, if ever he came to
Montebello. I have the chest in
safe-keeping. But I can only
give it to a person who can prove
he is the son. You see my problem?

TANCRED
I do. Right now, I do not need
money and jewels. I have many
things to do. But if ever I find
proof, I will bring it to you.

MAYOR
I see. So be it.

TANCRED
I wish to discuss something else.

I am looking for winter quarters
for my men. Could your town
provide billets and food? We pay
the standard rates and my men are
well behaved.

MAYOR
We already have such an
arrangement with another captain.

TANCRED
Oh?

MAYOR
Yes. Carlo Gonzaga.

TANCRED
Gonzaga!

MAYOR
Yes, Gonzaga. The town council
approved the idea - I was not
convinced - but so far it has
worked without problems..... In
fact, they are coming today to
discuss future terms. They
should be here by now.

He goes to the telescope and trains it on the
approach road.

MAYOR
There they are. See for yourself.

Tancred trains the telescope on the road and focuses, through the dust, on Gonzaga. A tall man, thin, hook-nosed, head held high.

Tancred moves the telescope to the left and focuses on the next rider. A very handsome young man, gaily dressed, armed with sword and dagger.

Tancred moves the telescope again. A second very handsome young man, with identical features to the first. Tancred moves the telescope back and forth to see if they are the same.

MAYOR
Gonzaga's sons. They are twins.

Tancred moves the telescope further to the left. He freezes.

MAYOR
Ah. You have seen the girl.

Tancred is riveted to the telescope. The dust clears and he sees a beautiful girl, swaying gently with the movement of her horse, pushing a strand of hair from her face.

                    TANCRED
Who is she?

                    MAYOR
She is Gabriella. Gonzaga's ward.
She is the daughter of a captain
who died in battle. Gonzaga took
her in his charge.

                    TANCRED
What beauty!

                    MAYOR
She is promised to one of his
sons. Perhaps it would be best
if you left now.

                    TANCRED
Why? I am not afraid to meet
Gonzaga!

                    MAYOR
I'm sure you're not. But it
would be inconvenient for me to
have two captains in the same room.

INT. THE DOGE'S APARTMENT, VENICE - EARLY
EVENING

Huge sculptured fireplaces, vast paintings of

Venice's triumphs on the walls. A very large
table used as a desk by the DOGE. Richly
tapestried armchairs dotted about.

The Doge, distinguished, hooded eyes, stern
expression, is given some papers by a clerk.
COMMISSIONER RONCALI, dark features,
clever - watches.

                    THE DOGE
          Ah. Captain Tancred is here.

                    RONCALI
          Captain?

                    THE DOGE
          He has taken command of his dead
          father's troop.

                    RONCALI
          He is only a lad, Excellency.

                    THE DOGE
          We must give him his chance.

                    RONCALI
          Why not transfer his men to
          Gonzaga?

                    THE DOGE
          Because I have good reports of him.

And if he is anything like his father....

RONCALI
Gonzaga would make better use of
the men. This Tancred has little
experience.

THE DOGE
That is why I shall give him a
task and see how he fares.
      (to the clerk)
Ask the Captain to come in.

Tancred enters, holding his satchel, and bows.

TANCRED
Most noble Lord.

THE DOGE
Captain Tancred. I was sorry to
hear of your father's death. And
I am glad you will continue to
command the troop.

TANCRED
Thank you, Excellency.

THE DOGE
Venice is willing to renew the
contract with your father. In

your name. The clerk will see to it.

TANCRED
Would it please your Excellency
to extend the contract. In one
particular?

THE DOGE
In what particular, Captain?

TANCRED
My troop would be more efficient
if I had more horses.

THE DOGE
We can discuss that.

TANCRED
My troop would be more
manoeuvrable-

THE DOGE
Captain. At this moment I have a
problem that requires early
attention. From you.

TANCRED
Yes, Excellency. Instruct me and
I will deal with it.

An amused expression flits across the Doge's face.

>   THE DOGE
>   There is a troop advancing into
>   the Veneto.   They have not asked
>   our permission. I wish that they
>   be sent off. There is no need
>   for a battle. Just a firm
>   discouragement. Please attend to
>   it, Captain. Their location is
>   shown on this map. Commissioner
>   Roncali will be in charge of your pay
>   and supplies.

EXT. ALONGSIDE A CANAL - EARLY EVENING

Tancred leaves the palace and walks along the path by a canal. He hears a scuffling noise and the clash of swords.

TWO MEN in black eye-masks are attacking PALMA, a slim figure dressed in grey. Palma defends himself well, in a showy manner.

Two further MEN in eye-masks run past Tancred. Tancred puts out his foot and trips one over, barges him into the canal.

He steps up to the third and taps him on the shoulder with his sword.

The man reels round, sword out. They fence back and forth.

Tancred manoeuvres his opponent so that his back is to the canal. Tancred lunges (his favourite lunge with grip turned inwards) and forces the man into the canal. He tries to climb out. Tancred pushes him back in with the point of his sword. The man swims off.

The first two men exchange glances and disappear into the darkness.

> PALMA
> Thanks, Captain. Two I can
> handle, but four maybe not so well.

They walk along the canal.

> TANCRED
> Do you know who they were?

> PALMA
> My ex-employer's cut-throats.

> TANCRED
> Your ex-employer?

PALMA

Yes. I just left him and he
thinks I stole some money. But
it was only back-pay. Which he
owed me.

TANCRED

He sent cut-throats after you
because you took your back-pay?

PALMA

Oh yes. Gonzaga is like that.
If he thinks you've done him
wrong, you're on his death list.

TANCRED

What was your job with him? What
do you do?

PALMA

I'm an accountant.

TANCRED

An accountant!

PALMA

Well. Accountancy is my job.
But my passion is fighting.

TANCRED

Really? So what are you going to
do now?

PALMA

Try and find another employer.
Won't be easy - especially with
Gonzaga after me.

TANCRED

I need an accountant. A fighting
accountant! We are a small troop,
now, but I intend it to be bigger.

PALMA

Then well met, Captain! I'm your
man. Count me in for any swordplay.
I'll do your numbers in between.
Keep the records. And deal with
your Commissioner.

They get into a gondola.

PALMA

By the way, who is your
Commissioner?

TANCRED

Roncali.

                    PALMA
         Ah. Roncali. Not good.

                   TANCRED
         Why?

                    PALMA
         He's Gonzaga's Commissioner, as
         well.

INT. COMMISSIONER RONCALI'S PALAZZO -
NIGHT

A large room, an immense mantelpiece, gilded
mirrors on the walls, gold candle sticks, a
DWARF in a corner, reading.

Roncali sits at a gold-rimmed table. Gonzaga
stands before him, drops his breastplate on the
floor.

He pushes a large bag of gold ducats across
the table and
sits.
                   GONZAGA
         Here is your percentage on last
         month's operations.

Roncali opens the bag, takes out the coins and
proceeds, lovingly, to make small stacks of
them, as they talk.

                    RONCALI
Most kind.

                    GONZAGA
Is there any news on when a
Captain General will be appointed?

                    RONCALI
There is no talk of it at the
moment. Things are relatively
quiet.

                    GONZAGA
Have you spoken to the Doge?

                    RONCALI
One does not speak to the Doge,
in the sense you mean it - one
waits for the right moment and
then tries to influence a decision.

                    GONZAGA
I'm getting impatient.

The dwarf brings wine and goblets, and serves
them.

                    RONCALI
                    (looking at the
                    gold before him)

Rest assured I shall do my very
best for you.

GONZAGA
When I am Captain-General, the
rewards will be uncountable.

RONCALI
Of course. Do you know of a
Captain called Tancred?

GONZAGA
The son of what's-his-name who
died recently?

RONCALI
Yes, him. The Doge is taking an
interest in him.

GONZAGA
Pah!. He's just a lad and his
troop is small.

RONCALI
True.

GONZAGA
The Doge is soft-headed. Do you
think it could come to anything?

RONCALI

I doubt it.

                    GONZAGA
I don't want him picking up any
serious business.

                    RONCALI
Don't worry. I shall neutralise
the situation.

                    GONZAGA
        Good.

INT. TANCRED'S TENT - DAY

Tancred, Siegfried and Palma study the Doge's
map, spread on a trestle table.

                    TANCRED
        Let's see where the uninvited
        troop is camped. It's marked here.

                    SIEGFRIED
        Oh ho! Do you see where they are?

                    TANCRED
        There?

They laugh uproariously. Palma stares at the
map.

A SOLDIER appears at the entrance.

> SOLDIER
> Beg pardon, Captain. Company.

Tancred and Siegfried step outside.

EXT. OUTSIDE TANCRED'S TENT - SAME TIME

Out of a cloud of dust and riding at a steady trot is a large group of armed men. They rein in, in front of Tancred. They are led by Guido Gonzaga. He looks about the camp with a sneer. Tancred nods briefly to the soldier, who leaves them.

> TANCRED
> Good day, gentlemen.

> GUIDO
> Captain Tancred?

> TANCRED
> Yes.

> GUIDO
> You are harbouring a fugitive.

> TANCRED
> Am I?

GUIDO
You are harbouring a criminal. A
thief.

TANCRED
Do we have any thieves here,
Siegfried?

SIEGFRIED
We are all thieves, Captain!

TANCRED
Surely not, Siegfried.

GUIDO
Don't play games with me! You
will release him into my custody.

TANCRED
I'm afraid I can't do that.

Guido's men loosen their weapons.

GUIDO
What? Why not?

TANCRED
I don't know who you're talking
about.

GUIDO
The thief is called Palma. As
you very well know! Where is he?

TANCRED
Palma? Where is Palma, Siegfried?

SIEGFRIED
Busy, Captain.

TANCRED
Busy?

SIEGFRIED
He is doing the accounts.

TANCRED
Ah. Yes. Then I'm afraid,
Captain... what is your name, by
the way?

GUIDO
Guido Gonzaga!

SIEGFRIED
(to Tancred)
Guido Gonzaga, Captain!

TANCRED
Indeed, Siegfried. Well, Captain

> Guido, as you see, I can do
> nothing. Palma is working.

Guido is by now furious and his men watch his
reactions.

> GUIDO
> Give him to me now! Or we shall
> take him!

> TANCRED
> You do not seem to understand,
> Captain Guido. I have told you
> he is busy. You may leave.

> GUIDO
> (over his shoulder
> to his men)
> Draw swords!

> TANCRED
> You have missed something
> important.

> GUIDO
> What are you talking about?

> TANCRED
> Look around you.

Guido turns in his saddle. His group is

surrounded by Tancred's archers, bows drawn.

                    TANCRED
          Siegfried. Ask the men to make a
          passage for Captain Guido's troop.
          They are leaving.

Furious though he is, Guido knows he must
retreat. He swings about and his troop follows
him off in a cloud of dust.

Tancred and Siegfried return to the tent.

INT. TANCRED'S TENT - SAME TIME

                    PALMA
          Thanks, Captain. Sorry to cause
          you trouble.

                    TANCRED
          That was no trouble.

                    SIEGFRIED
          None at all.

                    TANCRED
          Now. These uninvited troops.

                    PALMA
          Why were you laughing about them?

TANCRED
See their position on the map?
We know this area. The Doge wants
us to discourage them, but not to
start a battle. So we'll do just
what he wants. Eh, Siegfried?

SIEGFRIED
I'll get the men ready, Captain.
They'll enjoy this. Even though
it involves heaving rocks.

INT. THE DINING HALL IN GONZAGA'S
PALAZZO - NIGHT

The Hall is vaulted, sombre. Swords, shields
and banners decorate the walls. Furnishings
are heavy, uncomfortable.
Gonzaga, Gabriella and his sons, Guido and
NICCOLO, sit at
dinner.

GONZAGA
I intend to give a Ball.

The others look at him in astonishment.

GONZAGA
It is time Venice knew who is
going to be their next Captain
General.

                    GUIDO
Is it decided then, father?

                    GONZAGA
Not yet. But it will be soon.
The Ball will for Commissioner
Roncali.

                    NICCOLO
Is that wise, father?

                    GONZAGA
Wise?

                    NICCOLO
Well. In view of your
relationship with him. I thought
it was not meant to be common
knowledge.

Gabriella looks at him, questioningly.

                    GONZAGA
                    (irritated)
To the outside world, Niccolo,
the ball will be in honour of
Commissioner Roncali's wife. She
is also the Doge's cousin and may
be useful to me. So. Guido.
You have dealt with Palma?

GUIDO
Not yet, father.

GONZAGA
Why not yet? Did you find him?

GUIDO
Yes.

GONZAGA
Yes? Where is he then?

GUIDO
He has joined another troop.

GONZAGA
Another troop? Whose?

GUIDO
A captain called Tancred.

GONZAGA
Tancred? Tancred! Well? What
did you do? Did you go to see
this Tancred?

GUIDO
Yes, father. Of course!

GONZAGA
And?

GUIDO
They were too many for us. But -

GONZAGA
You understand, Guido. It is
important to me that Palma be
punished.

GUIDO
Do you think I am afraid? Eh,
father?

GONZAGA
Just do it! Also, I want this
Tancred out of the way.

Gabriella conceals her surprise at the way this
conversation is developing.

NICCOLO
Why is that, father?

GONZAGA
Because I wish it. We shall
invite him to the Ball.

NICCOLO
Will he come? He must know we

are against him.

                    GONZAGA
That is why he will come. And
that will give me the opportunity
to give him some advice.

He rises and leaves the table. The others
follow. They allow Gabriella to pass in front.

                    GONZAGA
              (looks at Guido)
Perhaps we shall announce your
nuptials at the Ball.

Gonzaga watches Gabriella. She says nothing.
He looks at Guido, shakes his head in irritation.

EXT. THE FOOTHILLS OF A VALLEY IN THE
VENETO - DAY

Tancred and his men heave and lever rocks
into a slow-running river.

They work quickly to divert the flow of water
which slowly spreads out and finds a new
course.

They complete their work and the spread of
water gathers speed.

They stand, point and laugh.

The water now runs fast toward a military camp set out in the valley.

Soldiers in the camp shout warnings to their mates but the water is at their feet and spreading through the camp.

The soldiers in confusion clutch their arms and armour, their packs, try to round up their panicking horses.

Tancred and his troop ride down on dry ground to the camp.

They stand in unfriendly silence and watch the soldiers.

The soldiers scramble away, watching Tancred's troop warily.

The soldiers' captain rides up.

                    CAPTAIN
          What is the meaning of this?

                    TANCRED
          Armed troops are not allowed in
          Venetian territory without
          approval. You have not asked for

permission.

                    CAPTAIN
Then damn Venice! I'll sell my
services elsewhere.

He pulls his horse's head round and gallops off.

                    SIEGFRIED
There's the mercenary for you.
If he knows he can't win, he
finds another employer.

                    TANCRED
I shall report to the Doge.
Palma, you can come with me and
organise provisions.

INT. THE DOGE'S APARTMENT - DAY

Tancred stands before the Doge.

                    TANCRED
.....and so they left, wet, and
without a single blow. As you
requested.

                    THE DOGE
Ingenious, Captain. Most amusing.
Perhaps they went to Milan. I
shall have more work for you

shortly. I will send word to
your camp.

                TANCRED
Would it please your excellency
to grant an addition to the
contract.

                THE DOGE
Ah, yes. Your earlier request.
What is it that you want, Captain?

                TANCRED
If I had more horses, my troop
would be more manoeuvrable. Speed
allows a commander to out-flank
an enemy. It allows him to make
the decisive blow.

                THE DOGE
The great Caesar would agree with
you. "The art of war is rapid
and audacious attack." How many
horse do you wish for?

                TANCRED
Fifty, Sire. If you so please.

                THE DOGE
Make it so. See Commissioner

Roncali. I expect good things of
you, Captain. Do not disappoint me.

TANCRED
I will not. You may rely on it.

EXT. ALONGSIDE A CANAL - LATER

Tancred and Palma leave the Palace square.

PALMA
The Commissioner is not best
pleased to give you those horses.
I'll wager Gonzaga won't be either.

TANCRED
I don't like that Roncali. I
doubt if he's honest.

PALMA
I shouldn't think so for one
minute. Do you know the painter
Bellini?

TANCRED
Only by reputation.

PALMA
I used to do his accounts. His
studio is along here.

TANCRED
A painter has accounts?

PALMA
It's big business. He has a staff
of fifty, at least. They produce
a lot of pictures.

Palma points the way into a large building.

INT. BELLINI'S STUDIO - CONTINUOUS

Palma leads Tancred through a series of rooms.
Tall ceilings, no furniture except a few benches.
Canvases, painted panels, wooden mannequins
leaning against the walls, trestle tables
supporting pots of paint mixes, easels standing
with work in progress,

Bellini's staff go about their work, mixing or
painting; most nod to Palma.

The end room is lit by a large window, an easel
stands diagonally to it. On the easel a portrait
of a girl, looking modestly down.

BELLINI is working on this portrait, glancing at
his model who is behind a screen. He turns
from the painting.

BELLINI
Ah, Palma! I'm glad you're here.

PALMA
How are you, Giovanni? This is
my friend - I should say,
employer - Captain Tancred.

BELLINI
Do you like paintings, Captain?

TANCRED
I have not had the chance to see
many.

BELLINI
If you don't mind, I need to talk
to Palma about an accounting
problem. Have a look at the
pictures. We won't be long.

Tancred looks at the portrait. He steps round it
and sees the model that Bellini is painting.

It is Gabriella. They stare at each other, clearly
stricken.

TANCRED
You are Donna Gabriella Gonzaga!

GABRIELLA
That is correct. Have we met?

TANCRED
No. I saw you and your brothers -
your half-brothers - at Montebello.

GABRIELLA
Oh, I see. You live there.

TANCRED
No. I was passing through. I was
with the mayor.

GABRIELLA
Will Bellini be long?

TANCRED
No. He needs a few minutes with
my colleague, Palma.

GABRIELLA
Palma? The accountant?

TANCRED
(surprised)
Yes. Ah. Of course. He worked for
your father.

GABRIELLA
My guardian. So you must
be....Captain Tancred!

TANCRED
Yes, I am.

GABRIELLA
The mercenary?

TANCRED
Yes. The mercenary. Like your
guardian. And your father.

GABRIELLA
(coldly)
You seem to know a lot of personal
details that should not concern
you, Captain.

TANCRED
Is someone here to escort you home?

GABRIELLA
What!

TANCRED
To accompany you to your home.

GABRIELLA
No. Yes. No! It would not be
appropriate for you to accompany
me anywhere, Captain.

TANCRED
May I ask why? The streets are
sometimes dangerous.

GABRIELLA
Firstly, because I do not need an
escort. Secondly, I hardly know
you. And thirdly, I cannot -

TANCRED
Cannot?

Bellini and Palma return. Tancred quickly steps
back in front of the portrait.

BELLINI
Do you like it? Now you have
studied it?

TANCRED
I think it is...exceptional. What
is it called?

BELLINI
It has no name at the moment. It

goes to a church in Bohemia

TANCRED
A long journey. And possibly
dangerous. There are brigands in
the pass. Allow me to arrange for its
escort. No brigands will attack
my men.

BELLINI
Well. Thank you. I must ask the
client if he wishes to pay for an
escort.

TANCRED
No need for that. I will do
it, freely, but for a small gift
in return.

BELLINI
What gift?

TANCRED
A copy of this portrait.

BELLINI
I shall have to ask the person
concerned.

TANCRED
Then I beg you to ask. If it can

be done, I am at your command.

He steps back so he can look round the screen before turning to leave.

EXT. A SQUARE WITH A BRIDGE OVER A CANAL - DAY

The square is crowded out, people lean from windows, throng balconies, packed gondolas bob side by side, red and blue banners flutter everywhere.

Either side of a broad wooden footbridge are two groups of young men, in parti-coloured shirts and tights, red and white, blue and white. They shout and jeer at each other.

A STEWARD stands in the middle of the bridge trying to make himself heard.

                    STEWARD
          No punching! No low blows! No
          gouging!

Tancred and a group of his men, with Palma and Siegfried, push their way through the crowd towards the bridge.

Siegfried wears a red and white shirt and white and red trousers. A huge cheer greets his arrival.

Tancred stares around him as though looking
for someone.

                    PALMA
          So the object is to push the
          other side off the bridge?

                    SIEGFRIED
          Exactly.

                    PALMA
          I see. Who leads the other side?

Another huge cheer. ORSO, built like a bear,
cropped hair and large beard, wearing blue and
white, joins the young men on the other side of
the bridge.

                    SIEGFRIED
          Him. Orso. Works for Gonzaga.

                    PALMA
          I've never seen him before.

                    SIEGFRIED
          He's always out at their camp.

                    PALMA
          Looks tough.

                    SIEGFRIED
He is. None tougher.

Tancred looks at him, amused.

                    STEWARD
                (moving off the
                bridge)
The parties will approach!

The two groups, led by Siegfried and Orso, trot
on to the bridge and stop in the middle.

Siegfried and Orso glare at each other.

                    STEWARD
I declare the bridge battle of
San Campo....commenced!

Each group closes in upon itself. Then they
come together with a thud. Heaving, pushing,
sweating, grunting. The two groups seem
evenly matched.

The spectators cheer and wave banners
furiously.

The reds push the blues back a little, the blues
push the reds back a little. Siegfried and Orso
are up front, red faced, straining and pushing,

shoulder against shoulder.
They heave and grunt in-between sentences.

          ORSO
You smell even worse than last
time.

          SIEGFRIED
Where did that filthy beard come
from?

          ORSO
I grew it, you dumb ox!

          SIEGFRIED
Who got wet, last year?

          ORSO
Can't remember.

          SIEGFRIED
Well, this year, both of us have
to.

          ORSO
Eh? Why?

          SIEGFRIED
There's a new tavern in the next
square. We should go there. Today.

ORSO
Good!   What's it called?

SIEGFRIED
The Golden Chair.

ORSO
So?

SIEGFRIED
It's run by a widow.

ORSO
So?

SIEGFRIED
She's called Violetta. What a
woman. What a build. Statuesque.
A real beauty!

ORSO
Oh ho!

SIEGFRIED
You should see her, Orso. Let's
get this over with and get round
there.

ORSO
We'll have to keep it going a bit

longer.

Tancred has seen the balcony where Gonzaga and Gabriella sit. He enters the next-door building.

INT. THE BUILDING - CONTINUOUS

Tancred pushes past spectators, mounts the stairs and squeezes onto a balcony. It is adjacent to Gabriella's. He gazes at her.

She feels his gaze, turns her face and sees him.

They pretend an interest in the bridge battle but their eyes keep returning to each other.

EXT. ON THE BRIDGE - CONTINUOUS

Siegfried and Orso are making Herculean efforts – or pretending to.

> SIEGFRIED
> Sideways manoeuvre?

> ORSO
> Can't see another way of finishing this. Did they clean the canal this year?

                    SIEGFRIED
I hope so. Anyway, I've got dry
clothes for us nearby.

                    ORSO
Everything organised, eh? You
must be smitten! Right then.
Heave on.

Siegfried and Orso push slowly sideways, crab-
like, to the edge of the bridge, taking their
respective groups with them.

The men at the edge of the groups fall into the
canal, one by one. The crowd cheers and jeers
as each man falls in.

Officials in gondolas attempt to rescue them.

Finally, both teams tip over the edge and
flounder in the water.

The crowd roars and laughs.

Siegfried and Orso haul themselves out onto
the quay, slap a few backs and disappear.

INT. THE BUILDING - CONTINUOUS

Gonzaga has noticed Tancred's interest in

Gabriella.

> GONZAGA
> Do you know that young man?

> GABRIELLA
> No....I do not.

> GONZAGA
> He seems to know you.

A voice from below shouts up.

> VOICE
> Hey, Tancred! Siegfried's given
> way!

> TANCRED
> No chance, my friend!

Gonzaga glares.

> GONZAGA
> (to Gabriella)
> Is he Tancred? Eh?

> GABRIELLA
> I.....don't know him.

> GONZAGA
> He's that damned Tancred, I'll be

bound. Where's Guido? Blast him!
Where is he?

                    GABRIELLA
He's with his friends down there.

Gonzaga locates Guido. Guido enjoys himself
with a group of men and girls in bright dress.

Gonzaga glares with frustration, looks round.
Tancred is gone.

INT. 'THE GOLDEN CHAIR' TAVERN - A FEW
MINUTES LATER

Gleaming copper pans hang from dark beams.
On a raised platform is an elaborately-carved
chair, painted gold.
Several customers eat and drink at solid tables.

One group is noisy, increasingly inebriated.

Siegfried and Orso stride in, sit and look
around.

                    ORSO
Where is she?

                    SIEGFRIED
Patience, my friend.

THE BOY approaches. About 9 years old,
cheeky look.

>   THE BOY
> Good morrow, gentlemen. What
> will be your pleasure?

Siegfried and Orso are amused.

>   SIEGFRIED
> Well, young sir, wine and food.
> Where is your mistress?

>   THE BOY
> I can take your order, good sir.
> Just advise me of it.

>   ORSO
> How can we order if we don't know
> what you offer? Young sir.

>   SIEGFRIED
> Yes. Perhaps the owner of this
> excellent tavern can acquaint us
> with your offering.
>   (to Orso)
> Elegant, eh?

>   THE BOY
> If you don't wish to order, you
> can leave.

Orso raises his hand to cuff the boy.

VIOLETTA, tall, statuesque, blond hair piled high, has approached unseen.

> VIOLETTA
> Lay a hand on that boy and you'll
> be out on your neck.

Siegfried and Orso jump to their feet and retreat, surprised, admiring.

Orso leans forward and pats the boy gently on the head.

> ORSO
> It was only a gesture, ma'am.
> Nothing serious.

> VIOLETTA
> Good. So what may I bring you?

> SIEGFRIED
> Red wine and cichetti, ma'am.

The boy runs off.

The noise at the drunks' table is increasing.

Violetta turns to go.

                    SIEGFRIED
          Er. Did you see the bridge
          battle, ma'am?

                    VIOLETTA
          The bridge battle? That boys'
          game?

Siegfried and Orso crestfallen.

Violetta appraises them slowly.

                    VIOLETTA
          Ah. I see. You're the two
          biggest boys. So who went in the
          canal, this time?

                    ORSO
          Both of us, ma'am.

                    VIOLETTA
          I thought there was a slight smell.

Two men, one small and one large, jump up
from the drunks' table and fight, rolling around
the floor, banging against tables, tipping up
chairs.

                    SIEGFRIED
          Shall we stop that for you, ma'am?

                    VIOLETTA
          No thanks.

She walks slowly over to the two struggling
men.

She lifts down a large copper pan from a
beam, slams it down on the big man's head.
He collapses.

She gets hold of the small man by the scruff of
his neck and his belt, throws him out the door.

Siegfried and Orso watch admiringly.

Violetta walks over to the drunks' table.

                    VIOLETTA
          Out! And take your fat friend
          with you.

                    A DRUNK
          Oh, Violetta! Can we come back
          tomorrow.

                    VIOLETTA
          All are welcome in my tavern.
          Sober.

They leave, sniggering. Violetta returns to

Siegfried and Orso's table.

> VIOLETTA
> Thank you for the offer.

The boy comes with wine and food. Violetta serves the wine. Siegfried and Orso are captivated.

Violetta sits. Siegfried and Orso's growing delight is watched by the boy with a resigned smile.

> VIOLETTA
> So. I can recognise soldiers,
> when I see them. Which troop are
> you with?

> SIEGFRIED
> I'm with Captain Tancred and Orso,
> here, is with Captain Gonzaga.

> VIOLETTA
> Never heard of them. But then,
> I'm new here.

> ORSO
> Where are you from?

VIOLETTA
Where I'm from is no business of
yours. Until I know you better.

SIEGFRIED
How did you know we are soldiers?

VIOLETTA
(smiling)
Look at you! Big brutes, muscles
everywhere, rough clothes,
unshaven, table manners few, a
smell. Easy. But, don't
misunderstand me. I like soldiers.
Their needs are few and well
known. You know where you are
with them.

Siegfried and Orso even more pleased.

ORSO
But we're not just soldiers.
We're in charge.

VIOLETTA
After the captains.

ORSO
Of course.

VIOLETTA
So you have money to spend?
Shall I bring more wine?

SIEGFRIED
If we may have the continued
pleasure of your company. Ma'am.

VIOLETTA
Very prettily put, Sergeant.

Violetta leaves them.

SIEGFRIED
Well?

ORSO
You were right. What a woman!
What a woman!

Violetta returns with a full bottle of wine.

VIOLETTA
A bottle of my best wine,
gentlemen.

ORSO
It's a handsome chair, your
golden chair. It looks foreign.
Where's it from?

                    VIOLETTA
        It was a gift.

The door to the tavern is thrown open. The
drunks have returned with re-inforcements.

                    SIEGFRIED
        Look at that, now.

                    ORSO
        There's a thing.

                    VIOLETTA
        I'll accept your offer this time,
        gentlemen. But don't let them
        damage my chair.

                    SIEGFRIED
        Why don't you move it out of the
        way?

                    VIOLETTA
        Because it's screwed down. Come,
        boy.

She and the boy stand back and watch.

During the brawl that follows, the golden chair
is in great danger of being hit by flying chairs,
staggering drunks, men who have been hit

hard or thrown by Siegfried or Orso; but each time, in the nick of time, it is saved by them.

Also at risk, but protected with great dexterity, is the bottle of wine which loses a few drops, but no more, despite being picked up, put down, and thrown between Siegfried and Orso at dangerous moments in the fighting.

The brawl continues until Siegfried and Orso are the last left standing - in front of the chair, Siegfried holding the wine bottle.

> VIOLETTA
> My!

> THE BOY
> Whew!

INT. THE DINING HALL IN GONZAGA'S PALAZZO - EVENING

Gonzaga and his sons dine.

> GONZAGA
> Where is she?

> GUIDO
> She said she wasn't hungry.

GONZAGA
Who were you with today at the
bridge battle?

GUIDO
Friends.

GONZAGA
You should have been with us.
You'll never persuade her if
you're always off elsewhere.
There was some young bravo making
eyes at her.

GUIDO
It won't be a problem. When I'm
good and ready.

GONZAGA
It won't, eh? We'll see. What
have you done about Palma?

GUIDO
Nothing yet.

GONZAGA
Nothing yet! Hellfire! Did I
not tell you to bring him back?
Eh?

                    GUIDO
          Yes, father. You did. And I
          will. Just leave it. I've told
          you I'll do it!

Gonzaga walks out in disgust.

                    GUIDO
          He'll drive me crazy with his
          damned Palma.

                    NICCOLO
          You'll have to do something.

                    GUIDO
          God damn! Don't you start!
          Anyway, I have something planned
          for both Palma and the clever
          Tancred. The night of the ball.
          You'll see.

EXT. A VALLEY THROUGH FOOTHILLS - DAY

A convoy of merchants' carts and laden mules
progresses slowly along a track of stones and
holes.

Some of Tancred's troop are riding point.
Tancred and Palma are at the front with a

merchant, DATINI.

> TANCRED
> When you have trouble with
> brigands, what do they want,
> merchandise or money?

Tancred looks up at the foothills. On either
ridge is a line of horsemen, keeping pace with
the convoy.

> DATINI
> They have no skill as merchants.
> They don't take our goods. They
> want money.

> TANCRED
> Much?

> DATINI
> Enough to have an impact on our
> profits.

> TANCRED
> They don't seem to be bothering
> you today.

> PALMA
> We've been tracked for a while
> now, Captain. On the ridge. Both
> sides.

TANCRED
I doubt they're brigands. They
look like stradiots.

PALMA
Stradiots?

TANCRED
Greek mounted warriors. Famous
for hit-and-run tactics.

DATINI
I don't like the sound of that.

TANCRED
Let's talk to them. We need a
piece of white cloth.

DATINI
Is that wise?

TANCRED
We'll see. Do you have a white
cloth?

DATINI
If you insist, Captain. I'll
fetch it.

                    PALMA
        I think they outnumber us.

                    TANCRED
        Tell the men. Bows at the ready.

                    DATINI
        Here's the cloth, Captain.

Tancred ties it to a stick, rides ahead of the
convoy, waves the white flag and shouts,

                    TANCRED
            Koubenta! Koubenta!

The horsemen stop, confer.

There is a shout and then both lines race down
from the ridges to join up in a dusty,
shuddering halt.

They are dressed in padded tunics and small
metal hats, and carry spears, pointed at both
ends.

The horsemen's leader, WELDA, trots forward.
He is young,wears a gold collar, lion's mane,
and is armed with spear, mace and dagger.

With him is an unarmed man in a robe, his

HERALD.

Palma joins Tancred.

              TANCRED
Greetings. I am Captain Tancred.

              HERALD
Here is Welda. Descended of
Alexander! Cunning as Achilles!
Swifter than Hannibal! Braver
than the lion, subtle as the fox!

Palma and Tancred exchange glances.

              HERALD
He sees like the lynx! He sweeps
down upon his enemies! Beware of
Welda!

Welda sticks his spear in the ground.

              WELDA
I Welda, Captain of Stradiots.

              TANCRED
Captain Welda, you are on Venetian
soil. Do you have permission to
be here?

WELDA
What mean you?

TANCRED
Venice requires all armed units
to ask permission to cross her
border.

WELDA
We are here to work.

TANCRED
Permission is still required.

WELDA
Why?

TANCRED
Because Venice is a peaceful
state and wishes to stay so.

WELDA
But you are soldier.

TANCRED
Where do you wish to work?

WELDA
Only for Venice.
(he spreads his arms)

We love peace!

His men raise their spears and shout war cries.

> WELDA
> (to his men)
> Eirini! Idioti!

His men stop shouting. They stick their spears
in the ground, adopt devout expressions.
Some cross themselves, ostentatiously.

> TANCRED
> You can work with me. I will
> speak for you with the Doge.

> WELDA
> You pay ducat for each dead enemy?
> We bring head?

> TANCRED
> No. I do not want heads. You
> will be paid the same as the rest
> of us. With a bonus for bravery
> in battle.

> WELDA
> Hah! There will be no bonus left
> for your men.

TANCRED
Then you will have truly earned
it, Captain Welda.

WELDA
Heh! Ducat not important. Welda
seek fame. Honour. More important
than ducat. What is my title?

TANCRED
Your title?

WELDA
Title. You Captain.
Welda need new title in Venice.

TANCRED
Caporale.

WELDA
What means?

TANCRED
'Capo' means leader. 'Rale'
means mounted troop.

WELDA
Ca-po-ra-le. Is good.

He leans forward in his saddle and kisses a

surprised Tancred on each cheek.

                    WELDA
          Now we are same side of border.

His men cheer and shout.

                    PALMA
          He's a cocky one, Captain.

                    TANCRED
          But did you see the way they rode
          down the ridges? They will be my
          light cavalry, Palma.

INT. GONZAGA'S PALAZZO - NIGHT

The ball is in progress. The rooms are candle-
lit by huge glass chandeliers, the walls are
decorated with flowers and tapestries, venetian
glass glitters on chests and tables.

Musicians play on a small stage, one sings
gaily.

The guests, gorgeously dressed, chatter, laugh,
move gracefully. Some eat off heavily-laden
tables lit by candlebras, wine is served in
goblets by retainers. A group of young men
and girls dance languidly.

Gonzaga works the crowd. Guido stands by a pillar, watching the entrance.

Tancred enters, hands his cloak to a servant.

Guido moves quickly to Gonzaga's side.

                    GUIDO
          He's here. That's him.

Gonzaga walks over to Tancred and stands in front of him.

                    GONZAGA
          Good evening, Captain Tancred.

                    TANCRED
          Good evening, sir. I thank you
          for your invitation.

Guido is talking quietly to two men in masks.

                    GONZAGA
          I hear you frightened off an
          unwanted troop. For the Doge.

                    TANCRED
          I was glad to have the opportunity.

                    GONZAGA
Well. Make it your last.

                    TANCRED
My last, Captain?

                    GONZAGA
You hear me. I don't want you
around Venice. I do the work the
Doge wants. All of it. Do you
understand me?

                    TANCRED
I understand the situation very
well, Captain.

                    GONZAGA
I'm glad to hear it. Enjoy your
evening. And stay away from my
ward.

He turns contemptuously away to welcome
more guests.

Tancred surveys the crowd. Nods to a few
acquaintances, bows to others.

He sees Gabriella and moves quickly to her.

TANCRED
Donna Gabriella, good evening.

GABRIELLA
Oh! What are you doing here? You
should not stay.

TANCRED
I only came for one reason. When
we met at Bellini's, you said you
could not allow me to accompany
you. Why was that?

GABRIELLA
You must leave!

TANCRED
Tell me why.

GABRIELLA
The reason is my own. It is
private. Please go.

TANCRED
I cannot.

GABRIELLA
You must!

Tancred takes her arm and moves her behind a pillar.

                    TANCRED
We are safe here.

                    GABRIELLA
No, you are not! Not here! Go!

                    TANCRED
Tell me, Gabriella, why I cannot
accompany you. Surely not because
of this disagreement with Guido?

                    GABRIELLA
Yes! No! Yes!

                    TANCRED
Is that all? Tell me.

                    GABRIELLA.
Then I will! My grandfather was
a mercenary. He was killed in
battle. My father was a mercenary.
He was killed too. I was only a
child. My poor mother died of a
broken heart. So I made a vow to
myself. Never, ever to have
anything to do with mercenaries.
There! Now you know.

                    TANCRED
But you live with this family of
mercenaries.

                   GABRIELLA
I have no choice. For the moment.

A musician starts to sing Stefano Landi's
beautiful "We all have need of Love".

Gabriella and Tancred stay still. The verses
mirror their situation.

Gabriella breaks her glance away, looks
around.

                   GABRIELLA
           Please go. For me.

She indicates that Guido is approaching.

Tancred bows to her, turns and bows to Guido,
brushes past him and leaves.

                     GUIDO
He won't be bothering you again.

Gabriella is perplexed.

EXT. ALONGSIDE A CANAL - A FEW MINUTES
LATER

Tancred walks along the quay leading away from Gonzaga's palazzo.

Several berthed gondolas line the quay wall, side by side. Tancred steps into one.

A crossbow bolt thuds into the wood of the gondola.

Two masked men appear, swords drawn. They leap into the gondola, attack Tancred.

Tancred retreats to the next one, drawing his sword. They press him and he jumps to the next gondola. The gondolas sway and dip, sword blades flash in the dark, Tancred keeps his balance, holds them off. He sees Guido watching from a corner.

Two more masked men run up, one has a crossbow.

A GONDOLIER jumps into the gondola alongside Tancred's.

> GONDOLIER
> Jump aboard, Captain, and we'll
> leave 'em behind.

Tancred lunges (his characteristic lunge) at his

two assailants, they retreat, he quickly joins the gondolier.

The gondolier expertly shoves off, rapidly leaves the quay.

The four masked men jump into two other gondolas and begin the chase. The gondolas race alongside quays, through narrow walls, under low bridges.

Tancred's gondola makes good speed, but the others won't give up. The crossbowman fires again and again but it is too dark to be accurate.

They near the Bridge of Sighs.

TANCRED
Come back and pick me up.

As his gondola passes under the bridge, Tancred grasps the iron under-structure and heaves himself up.

He drops onto the first of the pursuing gondolas as it passes under the bridge, knocks the men into the canal.

His gondolier has expertly turned back. Tancred jumps aboard. The gondola races off.

The assailants follow close, they won't give up.

The racing gondolas approach a junction with another canal.

> GONDOLIER
> Madonna just around the corner.

He swings the gondola round the corner, hugging a high wall. In the wall is a niche with a Madonna statue above a narrow shelf.

Tancred leaps onto the shelf. The enemy swing round the corner.

Tancred leaps onto their gondola, wounds the crossbowman, and punches the second man into the canal with the hilt of his sword.

His gondolier is back again and Tancred jumps aboard.

> TANCRED
> I'm almighty grateful.

> GONDOLIER
> Glad to be of help, Captain.
> Where shall I drop you off?

> TANCRED
> Here. Thanks.

He gets out, hands him a small purse.

>   GONDOLIER
>   No need, Captain. It's already
>   taken care of.

>   TANCRED
>   What do you mean?

>   GONDOLIER
>   The client has already paid.

>   TANCRED
>   What client?

>   GONDOLIER
>   The one who sent me to find you.

>   TANCRED
>   Someone sent you to find me? Who
>   was it?

The gondolier shoves off.

>   GONDOLIER
>   Sorry, Captain. Can't tell you.
>   Sworn to secrecy.

Tancred puts up his sword, shakes his head,
strides off.

Edward's Notes. Part 2.

Venice was an extraordinary place at the time this portrait was painted and Bellini was an important figure in it. I used to give talks to local societies about Venice and Bellini. If you're interested, you can read a couple of them here. You'll see there are references to the slides I used to illustrate the talks. The slides are on a CD but I can't find it at the moment. Anyway, here's the one about Bellini. Not as famous in our time as Titian or Leonardo or Michelangelo, despite the fact that he was a wonderful artist. You can see his beautiful stuff in the National Gallery.

Giovanni Bellini.

"Have you noticed", asks a guidebook of 1561, "that in Venice there are more paintings than in all the rest of Italy?"

If this was the impression that the visitor to Venice took away with him, then it was in no small measure due to the Bellini family and its workshop. A workshop that grew from modest origins to become one of the largest painter's ateliers anywhere, specialising in religious art, with numerous workrooms and studios and a gallery that became a literary and artistic venue. It was started by Jacopo Bellini in about 1430, continued by his elder son, Gentile, and then taken on to it greatest extent under his second son, Giovanni, who died in 1516. All three artists won huge renown and many commissions.

In the family tree, it is interesting to see that Jacopo's daughter married another famous artist, Andrea Mantegna.

We shall be looking at the workshop during its time under Giovanni, or 'Zianbellin' as he was affectionately known in the Venetian dialect.

In addition to the usual apprentices and studio hands, Giovanni employed at least a dozen lesser masters, generically known as the 'belliniani'. Here is a list of workers in the Bellini studio. Two of them were Titian and Giorgione.

In quantity, the greatest production of this and any other workshop in Venice would be portraits of the Madonna and Child. 80 have survived from Giovanni's workshop – they are in galleries today in New York, Detroit, Philadelphia and Washington; in Milan, Florence, Rome and of course Venice; in Berlin, Amsterdam, and in London, Glasgow, Birmingham and Southampton. How many others *may have been lost over the intervening 500 years especially when 15th. Century paintings were not in vogue?*

Giovanni is famous for his Madonna paintings, but equally for his 'sacra conversazione', and for his altar-pieces. John Ruskin said of the San Zacharia altarpiece by Giovanni: "It is one of the best pictures in the world", and he described Giovanni as "the last great religious painter"

But Giovanni's oeuvre is not just devotional painting; Kenneth Clark wrote "Bellini was one of the greatest natural landscape painters of all time. He was born with the landscape painter's greatest gift – an emotional response". This is high praise indeed when one considers that landscape painting, or the painting of nature, at that time, came in as the background to devotional paintings. As in the 'St Francis in the Desert', of which we can see some details.

When Albrecht Durer was in Venice, he wrote to a friend "Giovanni Bellini is very old, but still the best in painting." Ariosto came to the atelier and wrote a sonnet to Giovanni, describing him as "sublime artist, loving teacher"

Turner paid tribute to Giovanni – in a painting called "the pictures of Giovanni Bellini being conveyed to Chiesa Redentore", acknowledging his debt to the master of the painting of Venetian light and colour.

Bernard Berenson, in his pontifical manner, said that Bellini "led Venetian painting from victory to victory, and left it in the hands of Titian and Giorgione, an art more completely harmonised than any that the Western world had known."

In his 65 year evolution as an artist, Giovanni brought Venetian painting from provincial backwardness into the forefront of the Renaissance and the mainstream of Western Art. His work embraced religious, mythological and ceremonial material - and the growing demand for portraiture. Giovanni was an outstanding figure of the Quattrocento. And above all, he and his workshop were emblematic of the spirit of Venice.'

So that's the painter I so much admire and whose mysterious painting signed with a 'Z' I want to find.

And if you have the stamina for it, here's a talk I once gave about making a living in Renaissance Venice. But if you don't want to get into that kind of detail, then skip it! It's not hugely relevant to the Gabriella search.

Making a Ducat in Renaissance Venice.

The single, major factor that distinguishes Venice in the 1500s from the other powerful states in Italy is that it was not a principality or a dukedom, but was a state run by merchants, by traders and by businessmen.

The Venetian trading empire stretched down the Dalmation coast and into the Aegean. Her wealth was built on international trade and organised as a highly efficient state enterprise. Her galleys were constructed in the huge ship-building yards of the Arsenale and leased to private investors for each voyage. Routes were patrolled to avoid piracy and cargoes were strictly controlled to inhibit smuggling. The galleys sailed under the charge of a captain, who represented the investors, and a state-employed crew of sailors, oarsmen and carpenters, as well as a navigator, doctor, priest and book-keeper. Their cargoes would include glass and soap from Venice, German copper, Florentine cloth, amongst other European goods, and they would return with salt fish and furs from the Black Sea, luxury items from Constantinople, sugar, cotton and grain from Cyprus, silks and spices from the Levant, wheat and slaves from North Africa, wool and cloth from England and Flanders.

Venice was one of Europe's principal commercial ports and, with a population of over one hundred thousand (today it's seventy thousand) one of its largest cities. The Gran' Canale, lined with the houses of the rich merchants, snaked through the city, and spreading out from both banks was a maze of smaller canals, streets and passages, crowded with churches, small houses, apartment buildings, shops, stalls and taverns. Traders from all over Europe and the Middle East did deals in the business quarter by the Rialto Bridge (the only crossing over the Gran' Canale) and many settled in Venice. Some were numerous enough to form colonies - Germans, Greeks, Slavs, Jews, Armenians, Turks - creating a cosmopolitan environment remarkably conducive to transacting business with foreign countries.

The Doge's Palace, with its government offices, was the centre of political life and its occupants deliberately promoted an image of power, affluence and stability. The leading Venetians were at pains to create an environment, with carefully laid down rules and regulations, that all could see was not subject to the greed of an aristocracy, the whims of a princely family or the disruption caused by warring factions, each of which could devastate a carefully nurtured business, overnight. The government of Venice created an ideal environment for businessmen, selling, leasing or renting property, transport and services to them, as well as granting rights and opportunities and settling disputes. Venice provided an efficiently organised and, above all, safe and stable habitat.

Nonetheless, it was a state that supported a clearly stratified society. The Patricians, about 4% of the population, were firmly in control of the city and dominated political and cultural life. All important positions were held by patricians. Ambassadors, Captain Generals of the city's famous navy and the administrators of her colonies were invariably patricians. Every aspect of Venetian urban life was also in their control - the city's food supplies, the production and sale of salt, street and canal cleaning, rubbish collection, burials, the patrolling of the streets, passages, bridges and canals to curb the violence that was endemic in every European city of that time, as well as the upkeep of lighthouses and the maintenance of the breakwaters protecting the lagoon from the sea. Because of Venice's unusual structure and location, it was essential that these services function efficiently and the assumption of their responsibility at the highest level was deemed necessary by the

Venetians.

Below the patricians, but clearly distinguished from the mass of the working population, were the 'cittadini', the citizens, who formed about 10% of the population. Their status relied on proving long-term residency and at least two generations of non-manual trade. By livelihood, they were manufacturers, merchants, importers, doctors, lawyers, civil servants, for example, but they were excluded from political office. This class included the city's architects, sculptors and painters, for which Venice became justly famous.

For a long time there had been colonies of foreigners brought by the international trade - Greeks, Slavs, Dalmatians, Turks, Jews, Egyptians, Germans; 'the trade and profit of this state consisteth of all nations.' There were few prejudices. Various religions had their own churches. Foreigners with useful skills were encouraged to settle and if they brought with them a new process or an invention the State would encourage them to patent it or register a trademark.

There was no permanent garrison of troops -as in other cities of the time - to intimidate the population. It wasn't necessary. The Venetians of all classes felt that their government was a fair and egalitarian one. The religious fraternities, the parish organisations, the pageants and festivities gave them a feeling of belonging; and through the magnificence of the state architecture a feeling of pride.

If you fell upon hard times, the state would sell you bread and wine at subsidised prices. It provided hospitals and doctors and the Scuole (the religious fraternities) would take care of you if you were ill or penurious. There was hardly any unemployment. Beggars had to be registered and the number always rested around 400. If you were running a business, your enterprise was not at the mercy of tyrants or the whim of a Prince, nor your premises likely to be looted by marauding troops. Venice was an unusual and comfortable place to live in, for those times.

To avoid the opportunity for discord, the state organised and regulated in a benign manner. It provided street and canal cleaning, rubbish collection and burials. There were police patrols to keep drunken sailors and young hoodlums under control and maintain the peace at night in the Rialto taverns and hostels. The state provided a paid fire brigade as fire was a very serious matter. If you were a young woman in danger of assault, it was *better to cry 'Fire!' than 'Help!' More people would rush onto the street. The courts were considered fair and efficient. A young Patrician was gaoled for assaulting a black servant girl. If you couldn't pay a fine or a debt, you could work it off with labour service. Murder was a hanging offence. There was even legislation to curb bad language, insulting gestures and blasphemy. It generally succeeded, although less so with the gondoliers who were inordinately proud of their inventive vocabulary of insults.*

The appearance of the city to its residents at that time was of course marked by the canals, but also by a myriad of paths, lanes, alleys, streets, quayside footpaths, covered alleyways and bridges. The only bridge across the Grand Canal was the Rialto, with its shops and houses. It was a bustling business and commercial centre. But there were about 160 other bridges across the other canals. These were made of stone and wood, usually without handrails or side walls. The earliest bridges had ramps but after horses were banned, ramps gave way to steps. Pavements and bridges were laid out so as to enable you to get about in your own district - any journeys further afield were made by boat.

Community life centred around the 72 parish

churches, each with its campo or square, a well for drinking water and a market. Houses and apartment blocks, with external staircases, would be used at ground level for shops, workshops and kitchens with living quarters above. A large number of buildings had glass windows, which astonished foreign visitors. The campo was 'home territory', one's neighbourhood, often described as 'entro i ponti' - between the bridges. The bridges would take you over the boundary canals and into adjoining neighbourhoods.

Her local campo was a place where a woman could, in total freedom, appear in public, see her neighbours, chat, do her shopping, accompany her children and so on.

Many of the streets and campi were bricked or paved. One visitor observed: 'the city is as clean for walking in as a gracious chamber, so well paved and bricked it is.' He went on to note: 'the city is so well ordered and arranged that however much it rains in winter there is never any mud, and in summer no dust. The sea rises and falls there and cleans out the filth from the secret places.' A French Ambassador called the Grand Canal 'the most beautiful street in the world.'

The Gallery in Albemarle Street.

The next morning I walked round to the gallery.

In Albemarle Street, you pass a number of art galleries and if you look in the window the same scene presents itself: a couple of choice paintings up front, a number of others on the walls, each lit by a spotlight, and a sleek sales-person sat working at a desktop computer. A bell on the door to ring before they let you in. Nothing is priced, of course. Alongside each picture is just the name of the artist and the title he or she has given to the work. The contemporary works on view are unfathomable. You'll be given a wordy description of the artist's intentions if you go in and express interest.

But Edward's gallery, as always, impressed me. Large windows, again choice pictures up front but, inside, a relaxing environment of burgundy-coloured walls with paintings well spaced out and a few chairs and coffee tables in the centre of the various alcoves. When I had negotiated the complicated codes of the alarm system, I took a leisurely look around inside. The paintings were quite clearly what you would call old masters, even if they weren't the well-known names. There were paintings on dispay by Niccolo Rondinelli, Bartolomeo Veneto, Giovanni Martini, Mario Basaiti.

The bell rang. It was Dobri, with a tall, thin man, dressed in black, with a black beard and black hair in a pony-tail. Dobri introduced him as Boulton. 'The finder.'

"Any coffee about?" he asked. Dobri said he'd go out and get some.

"Plan to keep the place going?" asked Boulton.

"Probably," I answered. "But obviously it depends on if we can keep the stock coming in. How easy is it?"

"You need luck," he said and laughed. "Plus a bit of nous. There's plenty of Edward's second division paintings in Eastern Europe, but winkling them out is the tough bit."

"Where do you go looking?"

"Mostly out in the countries that once were part of the Austro-Hungarian empire. I've found some good stuff in Szekszard and Kaposvar. Where, as it says in the tourist leaflet, 'the Trans-Danubian mountains meet the Great Hungarian Plain.' Loads of good art was bought by the rich Austro-Hungarians way back when. Then when the commies took over after the Second World War, it was hidden before it could disappear into the KGB coffers. Families who have inherited it now want to sell it and travel in the West. Trouble is I have to deal with some regular oddballs who have figured out they can be profitable middle-men. Art and antiquities' theft is the fourth biggest global crime. How about that! Still, I reckon we can avoid the bad guys and there'll still be a good bit left for us!"

We drank coffee and I looked more closely at the paintings.

"Do you know much about art?" asked Dobri.

"Not a lot. I've been to a lot of galleries, but I'm not an expert, by any means," I admitted.

"Hey," said Boulton. "I came across something interesting in Liberech. A grotty town near Prague. One of the oddballs is offering a small collection of what he calls baroque pictures. Says they could benefit from restoration but assured me they would be a good price. I haven't seen them but he gave me a list. Basically a half-dozen smallish paintings, mostly landscapes but two portraits, one of a girl."

"There were many portraits of girls in the Baroque period," said Dobri.

Boulton raised his eyes to the heavens. "I know that, mate, but one of these portraits is signed with a single initial. He says it's an 'L'. Interesting, eh?"

"You mean it could be a 'Z'?" Ben said.

"Ah ha! You already know about Edward's famous quest. Anyway, I reckon as you're a Czech, Dobri, you should go. Maybe you'd like to go, Ben?   What d'you say?"

"Prague was my next port of call before I got the news about Edward," I said.

"Really? What for?"

"Work."

"If it's not indiscreet, what do you do for a living?" asked Boulton.

"I'm what's known as an issues manager."

"What's that?"

"I specialise in foreign and export problem solving. If a company has a problem overseas or with its export business, I can get called in to fix it."

"A trouble shooter? Have iPad, will travel?" I can't count the number of times I've heard someone say that.

"So you have a job to do in Prague?" continues Boulton.

"I have a client who wants me to find him a distributor."

"So you could check out the paintings while you're there?" asked Dobri.

"Certainly. Although it would be better if one of you were there with me. To ensure we're looking at real pictures and not some of those wonderful copies they do over there."

"When do you have to go?" asked Boulton.

"Soon as possible."

"Well then, you'll have to go, Dobri. I've got a friend coming over to London this week." said Boulton.

"No problem," said Dobri.

"OK? I'll give the guy a call and let him know he'll be hearing from you about a meeting. Look, I'll have to push off, now. I'm taking a ravishing girl from Mercerea-Cinc round the Nat Gall. And after that I'm taking her to see 'The Beggars' Opera.' I managed to get seats, would you believe."

"Go on, then," said Dobri. "Tell us where Mercerea-Cinc is."

"Gotta go. See you later."

I asked Dobri if Boulton had been a finder all his life.

"Not at all. When he left university he became

a political researcher working for some ambitious MP at Westminster. Eventually he gave it up. Couldn't stand the hypocrisy, he said. And he wanted to work for himself. He wrote some funny skits about life in politics under the last government, for TV and radio. And skits about art. You can read them on a website called johnproblem.com   He used a pen-name 'Jason Briggs'. Then he spent several years doing I don't know what in Eastern Europe before turning up at Edward's antique shop. That was before this of course," he said, looking round the gallery.

"Edward asked me to come round and meet him. We didn't know what to make of him. He produced a few small paintings which he offered to us. They were in scuffed old wooden frames, rotting cloth on the backs, filthy dirty and lots of old varnish. A tough job for a restorer. Fortunately, there was very little flaking on any of them and only a few small tears in the canvas. Edward was intrigued and said I should try and clean them up. Took me a while, I can tell you. They turned out to be two paintings by Pietro da Messina, one by Girolamo da Santa Croce, and three by Benedetto Codo. All Venetians. Edward was naturally thrilled out of his mind. He asked Boulton where he'd found this treasure. Boulton tapped his nose and said if we wanted more he would be happy to oblige. Well, who could refuse? So we agreed a modus operandi and we've never looked back. Edward asked him if he wanted to be a partner or something similar; to be a part of the business, but he said he was happy cruising around and finding stuff. So there you are; that's basically how the gallery now operates."

"I see it's now twelve o'clock and there hasn't been a single customer," I said.

"It doesn't work that way. Most of the time the serious customers came by appointment after Edward had located them, or they had heard of us and got in touch. He used to give them the full treatment. His charm, his specialist knowledge, and a particular way of presenting the painting that he thought would be the one for the client. Come over here and look at the Presentation Room, as he used to call it. Edward was not trying to go over the top with his clients. He just loved to make them feel that buying a painting was a big experience. Emotional, aesthetic, and not just an investment."

The Presentation Room was a smaller room, lined in dark maroon velvet, with two armchairs placed facing the far wall on which a painting hung in full illumination from two spotlights. By the door was a small table with drinks.

"God, this really reminds me of him. Not good.

Well. Let's go and get a drink. We usually did at this hour. And a sandwich."

W went down Albemarle Street and back to the bar in the Ritz and talked about the gallery and Edward and the art market.

"Did you always use this bar," I asked him, eventually. "Seems a bit pricey. The cost of a sandwich would buy a new shirt."

"Yes, we did. Edward had some kind of sentimental reason for being here, I think. Maybe an old romance although why he would bring anybody here in the first place, I don't know. Of course, the dining room is a knockout. But now we have a special reason to come here, thanks to Edward. Before he died he left a tab here for us to order from. Said he wanted us to remember him and drink Bellinis as we used to. He swore the staff to secrecy and told us to eat and drink until it ran out. Amazing guy."

"Well, here's to him," I said, raising my glass. "I wish I'd had more time to spend with him, but my job always had me travelling around overseas."

Edward's Notes. Part 3.

I've spent a lot of time on this pursuit, but it would have taken forever if I hadn't been able to use the resources of the web. The most astonishing stuff is available. On days when the girls were unable to come into the gallery, I would sit at the desk and google every possible way of tracking the portrait of the mysterious Gabriella.

You can find wills dating back to the 1500s, auction sale catalogues, obscure diaries, letters, unpublished monographs, unexpected bits of knowledge, almost everything! In fact it was from a catalogue of an auction that I found the next reference to the portrait. An auction that took place in 1570 in Paris at which the following item was sold:

'Un tableau d'un pied de haut sur 10 pouces representant une jeune fille (la Madeleine?). Ce portrait est d'autant plus curieux, qu'il est d'un coloris & d'une vivacite de pinceau admirable. Signe 'Z'.'

The 'Z' signature was a wonderful find. And the reference to admirable colouring and vivacity made me think immediately of Bellini.

I now knew that the portrait measured twelve inches by 10 (curious how the French were using feet and inches then) but not what the young woman looked like other than the comment that she might be Mary Magdalene. I'm not sure what use to me that was, but Bellini painted a Mary Magdalene in his picture 'Madonna and Child with Two Saints' in which he portrays her as a young Venetian girl complete with crimped and blonded hair. (They blonded their hair by sprinkling lemon juice on it and then sitting in the sun....)

I couldn't find any means by which the portrait ended up in an auction in France a hundred years after it was painted. Maybe it got sold by the original owner or given away or handed down - I don't know. But from there on the chase got clearer. I was able to find out who bought the picture at the auction. It was a Lord Mielding, an elderly, wealthy English aristocrat. Lord Mielding was a catholic and considered it too dangerous to live in England where they burnt non-protestants, so he exiled himself to France, having transferred much of his treasury and taken with him:

'An tall case wherein is a feather-bed and a bolster, in the same an pillow, an head-piece and my fox gown; an joined case with four pair sheets and pillow-cases and coverlet and

quilt, an jacket of silk, one of blanket, an quail cage....'

Clearly Lord Mielding liked his creature comforts. When he died, his will showed that he left the picture to his grand-daughter:

'I do gyve and bequeath unto my grand-daughter Judyth three pictures, one of the Madonna and Child by Catena, a drawinge of two hartes in a streame by Bonting, and third a portrait of a young ladye, marked wyth a sign Z.'

Unfortunately, back in England his grand-daughter's husband, the 3rd Marquis of Cadname, despite being protestant, was a rake-hell, developed the pox and gradually dissipated his entire fortune at cards, on the horses and with foolish investments. His wife put up with him for many years and finally walked out. Literally. Leaving him sitting in a drunken stupor with his friends, throwing dice in the drawing room of their home, Cadname Old Hall. After which he disappeared and his remaining effects were sold off. Not at a fancy auction but in the equivalent of a fire-sale. There are documents covering this in the local town archives. But they don't specifically mention the picture....

So, now, it appeared that the portrait was in Elizabethan England. But where? In a stately home? Lost? Perhaps in a church? It seemed impossible to know.

Many paintings seem to disappear for centuries. Even Bellini's most famous painting, 'St. Francis in the Desert', was lost to view until 1857, when a Captain Dingwall (try googling him - nothing!) exhibited it in Manchester. It was bought by Thomas Holloway, a famous pill manufacturer, who made a fortune selling what he described as the best remedy known in the world for diseases. He was the first to use newspaper advertising and in his ads listed the diseases his pills could cure. They ranged from asthma to worms by way of dropsical swellings and scrofula....

Later it was acquired by Henry Clay Frick, an American coke and steel magnate, who put it in his museum in New York, the Frick Collection, where it remains to this day. Try and see it if you can. It is marvellous...... a rendezvous with the sun, in a landscape painting which renders every aspect of nature full of charm and interest, from a rabbit peeping out between rocks to vines growing on a trellis, a shepherd with his grazing sheep and a city in the far background. Four feet by four feet of unadulterated delight.

Frick, by the way, was known as 'the most hated man in the US' for strike-breaking at his factories. He famously called in armed guards at one strike and the guards opened fire on the strikers. Goes to show that art appreciation is not always associated with a gentle nature....

Another famous Bellini painting , the 'Christ Carrying the Cross' - an astonishing portrait of Christ which was frequently said to work miracles - is on display in yet another wealthy American's museum: in Isabella Stewart Gardner's galleries in Boston. It was her favourite painting and to this day, under the terms of her will, a single rose is placed below it every morning. This famous lady was a baseball and prize-fight fan.....

But to get back to Gabriella, where was she now?

Cheapside, London 1590.

In a small room sits a young man at a desk, writing. His pen squeaks across page after page. He writes as fast as he can dip the quill in the inkwell. His concentration is complete, although now and then a smile passes briefly over his features and occasionally he leans back and stretches.

 A small dog sits at his feet. A mongrel of no easily determined ancestors, brown and black with a white patch around one eye. Every now and then the dog raises an eyebrow and looks up at the young man. Seeing him still busy with his scribbling, the dog utters a brief sigh, closes its eyes.

 Another young man looks in the door, sees the writer completely absorbed in his task, shrugs his shoulders and leaves. The frantic squeaking of the quill on the thick pieces of paper continues. The young man now has a look of growing triumph on his face and starts to scribble faster.

The dog gets up, stretches luxuriously from front to back, wags its modest little tail and barks.

"Unmannered dog," says the young man abstractedly. The dog barks again.

"Away, unpeaceable dog." mutters the young man. The dog barks again.

"Away, thou issue of a mangy dog!" shouts the young man, looking round. The dog wags its tail happily and puts its feet up on the desk. It knocks some of the papers to the floor and stands on them.

"Out, dog! Out, cur! Thou drivest me beyond the bounds of patience!" bellows the young man, pulling out his papers from under the dog. The dog licks his face, puts a paw on the young man's foot.

"O, be thou damn'd, inexecrable dog!" shouts the young man, pushing it away. The dog trots off. The young man returns to his writing. His quill takes up its squeaking, the pile of written papers grows. The dog puts its head on one side and watches attentively. Then it barks.

"Let gallows gape for this dog! You bawling,

blasphemous, incharitable dog! Would thou were'st a spaniel with head hung low and ears that sweep the morning dew away," shouts the young man over his shoulder At this, the little dog looks unutterably sad. It whimpers and slinks away to a far corner.

 "How now! Where's that mongrel?" demands the young man. The dog bounds back, tail wagging, slithers on the tiled floor and bangs into the young man's desk. The inkpot tips over, ink runs onto the floor. The dog backs swiftly away.

 "Oh! Hell-hound! I'll spurn thee hence!" shrieks the young man. The dog runs off and crouches down, its chin resting on the floor, watching the young man carefully. The other young man appears at the door again, looking impatient.

 "Come on," he says. "They wait upon us at the theatre. Have you finished that scene?"

"I have," Is the pleased reply. "I've got some good lines for Antony. About Havoc and dogs of war. Where is that over-weening mongrel?" The little dog is sat by the door, quivering in every limb with anticipation.

"Come, cur! Nature teaches beasts to know their friends, eh?"

The little dog rushes to its master's side, tail wagging furiously.

"You know, Ben, I would not lose that dog for twenty pound," says Will to his friend.

"Truly? Then I'm sure I do honour the very flea of your dog. Is that painting yours?"

"What painting?"

"There be only one painting, Will. There. On the wall behind you. A girl's head."

"No, it's not mine. The landlord's, I expect. Are we away, or not?"

Edward's Notes. Part 4.

Well, as far as I was concerned at that stage, the search had reached a dead end. And, for all I knew, the painting might no longer exist. But, out of the blue, I had a piece of unexpected luck.

When I was researching for my Venice lectures, I wanted to put in some detailed stuff about her merchants and their types of trading - quite naturally, as this was what Venice lived on in the Renaissance; business, commerce, trading, import/export, etc.

I wanted to show connections between Venice and England. London, Southampton and even Sandwich figure large in those trading relationships and are easily researched. But what got me going again on the search for Gabriella was that I came across some accounts stored in the British Library. Business accounts which had been kept by an agent in London who worked on behalf of merchants, both storing their goods and arranging sale where appropriate.

They had acted on behalf of a merchant called Grotius (I don't know his nationality), and they sold some of his merchandise to an Abyssinian merchant and importer called Khalid. Which information was dutifully recorded in their books. Among the items bought by Khalid was listed 'portrait of young woman, 14 inches by 10 inches, oil on canvas, unsigned but marked in lower right hand corner with a 'Z'. What a find!

Gin Lane, London. 1720.

They make an incongruous couple, Grotius and Forlan, as they pick their way along Gin Lane. Grotius is a stocky figure, strong and confident, dressed soberly with sensible boots, while Forlan is slight, although tall, and decked out in silks and folderols, twirling a cane as he walks along one pace behind Grotius.

"Hold on to your purse, Master," says Forlan. "They can steal it away and replace it with one full of counterfeit coins, whilst you don't feel it."

Grotius looks at him pityingly. "Do you really believe that?"

"No," says Forlan.

They have come from Covent Garden, walking along Henrietta Street and turning into Gin Lane, making for The Strand. Gin Lane is filthy, dirty gutters, wretched houses with broken windows, ("Beware the slops, Master," says Forlan), windows patched with rags and paper and, out behind, hideous stinking drains and latrines with, behind them, the dark hulk of Newgate Prison. The only building in good repair is the pawnbroker's shop, its windows heavily barred.

A drunken woman sprawls on the pavement while her child picks about in the gutter. A man fights with a dog for a bone. Old men, drunken, besotted, stagger by. Wretched, broken-down, miserable women shuffle along. A group of young men standing on a corner look at Grotius and Forlan, with feral eyes, move forward, but then hesitate. Grotius and Forlan step round a drunken fight between labourers in the gutter. A man dressed like a parson stands in the middle of an ill-coloured puddle reading loudly from a tattered bible.

In a doorway is a group of young women. They have rouged cheeks, matted hair and are dressed in scant and dirty apparel. One of them approaches Grotius.

'Very well, sir," she says. "You are here and so am I. What say you then?"

Forlan lifts his cane and pushes it into her stomach. "Let your business be whatever it will, but leave us," he commands. She trots along beside them.

"Come, sir," she says. "Why, this is a civil gentleman and cannot he answer for himself?"

"Do not be more stupid than you are, woman," says Forlan. "Go now, before I call the magistrate."

"Call the magistrate! In Gin Lane!" she cries, and laughs in his face.

Grotius stops and looks at her. He sees a dirty face, of no beauty, not even pretty, but with a certain determination and spirit. Not yet destroyed by the years of poverty no doubt to come. He pities her and knows that this is not a good reason to be kind.

"Let her come with us," he says. Forlan says "Surely not, Master. 'Tis a harlot, simple."

Grotius says nothing and strides on. A young man blocks his path.

"And what kind of a man are you, sir? Eh? This young lass is my sister. What would you have with her, eh?"

Grotius looks at Forlan and says "This fellow may delay my business this morning."

Forlan steps up to the young man.

"Do you wish, sir, to continue this folly? Or do you wish to see your mother again tonight? She would regret it greatly were you not to kiss her cheek again. Think on't." He shoots his cane out at the young man.

The girl says "Oh, shove off, Bart, and leave me alone. Go! Do!"

Bart replies, "Make it pay, girl." And walks off laughing.

Forlan says "Master?" Grotius says "Leave him."

Before they had left Rillstein's house, where they had spent the day comfortably, Rillstein had warned them, "In Gin Lane, the young woman will come and when you show interest in her, then comes a blood who says she is his sister and then come his friends to rob you."

"It's an old act," Forlan had said, twisting the handle of his cane and looking at the blade inside.

"Are you back tonight, Grotius?" Rillstein had asked. "There is the new opera. It's called 'The Beggars' Opera'. Particularly enjoyable after a walk through Gin Lane, they say."

"It will depend on my business," Grotius had replied.

They reach the end of Gin Lane and turn into The Strand. Here all is light and brilliance. Cleaner. Ornamented parapets, illuminated clocks, plate glass windows surrounded by stucco rosettes, gas lights glinting in richly gilt burners, finely dressed men, showily dressed women. The hum of many voices issues from the gin-shops on either side - elegant saloons with French-polished mahogany bars. Grotius strides on down towards Charing Cross. Forlan and the girl follow, she marvelling at the women's dresses. Forlan is singing to himself;

"Ye walkers all that youthful colours wear, Three sullying trades avoid with equal care;

The little chimney-sweeper skulks along, and marks with sooty stains the heedless throng;

The dustman's cart offends thy clothes and eyes, when through the street a cloud of ashes flies;

Protect thy shoes and coat; resign the way; And shun the surly butcher's greasy tray."

Opposite the stone cross, Grotius turns into a large, glittering gin-shop. The bar, elegantly carved, extends the whole width of the long wall and on each side there are great casks, painted green and gold, enclosed within a brass rail and labelled for the different varieties of gin, 'Old Tom 549', 'Young Tom 360', 'Samson 1421'. Beyond the bar, is a lofty and spacious saloon. On a counter in the middle are little baskets of cakes and biscuits, continuously renewed by a garishly dressed woman wearing a faded feather hat.

Forlan looks around admiringly. One wall of the saloon is hung with a jumbled collection of bric-a-brac and military paraphernalia. Swords and lances (all firmly secured), breast-plates, shakoes, copper pans and pots, a few small paintings in dirty wooden frames, pieces of textile with Arabic writing, a saddle bag and, proudly situated in the middle, a poor but colourful painting of a mounted soldier.

Grotius walks purposefully through the saloon to the back and knocks at a door marked 'Office'.

Forlan and the girl sit at a table and he orders a half-quartern of gin and peppermint.

Forlan says "Art hungry?" She nods. Forlan orders soft biscuits. When the gin arrives, the girl dips her fingers in it and wipes her face clean. She sips from her pot.

"Ugh!" she says. "I don't like that!" Forlan sighs and beckons the waiting-woman.

"Does your Old Tom have all the right herbs in it?" he asks.

"Oh yes, sir. All of 'em is present."

"Then bring us a pot," says Forlan.

"What 'erbs is that, then," asks the girl.

"Juniper, angelica, coriander, cardomon and orange peel," Forlan tells her. "You will like that, I warrant."

"I dunno," she says, dubiously. "Still. 'Tis a frolick, mister. Bein' with you, 'ere."

Grotius knocks again, harder. The door is opened by a thin fellow with sandy whiskers, wearing a fur cap to one side of his head.

"Yiss?" he says squinting at Grotius. "Ah! Is it Mr. Grotius, sir?"

"I am he. And you, I collect, are the Captain's brother-in-law? Is the Captain here?"

"No, Mr. Grotius. 'E's gorn away."

"Gone? Where?"

"'E's a gorn to the colonies."

"To the colonies? Which one?"

"Virgineeyah in the Americas. Gorn to make 'is fortune, 'e said."

"Indeed?" says Grotius.

"Yiss, sir, but 'e did say as how 'e was indebted to you and what a fine and civil gentleman you was, but 'e got in a sad pickle over a sword fight, wot 'e won of course, and so 'e went."

"Who is in charge now?"

"Me and 'is wife, my sister."

"I don't think I have made that lady's acquaintance."

"That's 'er, in the fevvered 'at."

"Well. I am here to collect the final part of payment owing to me for the provision of 47 barrels of best genevers to the Captain. A debt which is now one month overdue. Did he leave payment with you?"

"Not exackerly, Mr. Grotius. No. But 'e did leave you a inventry. Excuse me whiles I get it." Grotius turns, glances at Forlan and the girl.

" 'Ere we are, sir. The inventry! All writ up wonderful."

"What use is it to me?" asks Grotius.

"Well. The Capting offers you all the items on that wall as part payment of 'is owings to you. An' 'e 'oped you, bein'g a 'onest and sober gentleman, would not think that you 'ad been robbed by 'im, which considers 'imself a friend and 'opes to see you again under better circystances. An' 'e draws up the inventry of the items, all square and legal like."

Grotius takes the inventory and approaches the wall. Looks carefully at the various items, takes a small painting off the wall and turns it over, looks at the back, turns back a corner edge of the backing cloth. Replaces it on the wall.

"Is you Mr. Grotius, sir?" It is the lady in the feathered hat.

"At your service, ma'am."

"I warrant there's good value in some of those items, sir. Would you not say so?"

"I shall have my agents retrieve them shortly and then we shall see where they can be sold profitably. I shall advise you truthfully of the amount of my profit and how much that leaves owing by your husband. These are mostly curios with a limited market. They are not select artefacts, ma'am."

"Oh," she says. "Oh. Then you might, as a gentleman, Mr. Grotius, let me keep the picture of my husband on his charger. He looks so fine and it will do me good to see him there every day whilst he is away, sir."

"With pleasure, ma'am. On one small condition."

"Oh, thank you, sir! What small condition might that be?"

"That you take that girl over there in employment."

"Oh, bless you, sir, but we get twenty girls a day asking for employment! We cannot afford the dress and the food for a girl, no matter how hard she work!"

"I shall make it easier for you. I shall give you money for her clothes. I shall have that disappointing painting of your husband improved by an artistic acquaintance of mine for your personal greater pleasure. Which will also make it more valuable. In three months' time we shall come for the girl and take her away. Does that suit?"

"Well. I suppose.... I suppose I could use her.

Just three months, you say, Mr. Grotius?"

"Yes. However, when I come, she must be in fine health. And have not been abused or ill-used by either your customers or your brother. Do you agree, ma'am?"

"Oh yes, sir."

"If she has been, then I shall take her away and sell her in Africk."

"Sell her in Africk! You could not do it! Surely not, sir?"

"I most certainly could. And the guilt for that would be on your head. And your brother would be punished by my man Forlan."

"Oh, sir! Don't you trust me?"

"I trust no-one." He gestures to Forlan. "Bring the girl."

"What is your name, girl?"

"Nance."

"Listen carefully, Nance. You are to stay and work here for this lady who will house you, feed you and look after you for three months, when I and your friend Forlan will return for you. No harm will come to you. But if you drink one drop of gin during that time, I will know of it and will not come for you. Do you agree?"

The girl is numbed by what is happening and nods feebly, looking for re-assurance to Forlan. He smiles at her, touches her shoulder.

Out in the street, Forlan says, "So I'm her friend, am I?"

"I observed she was interested in you and you in her." replies Grotius.

"Where to now, Master?" asks Forlan, twirling his cane.

"We must go to Hartshorn Lane, near the river," replies Grotius, striding out once more. "To give the inventory to my agents."

"Why did you offer to improve the painting of that man who owes you money, Master?"

"Before I was a merchant, I did some soldiering and he and I were friends. He was a good fellow, unafraid and brave. But wild. And our ways drifted apart until I sold him the gin."

As they walk down towards the river, Forlan sings to himself, "There is a lady sweet and kinde, Was never face so pleased my mind......"

 The sun is down behind the roof of the Opera when they return to Rillstein's little house in the Garden. He has a visitor whom he introduces.

"Khalid is a Christian from Abyssinia. I asked him to stay because you may be able to offer him assistance in his business in London."

"In Abyssinia, peoples want geegaws and gimcracks from Europe," says Khalid. "For we Christians, paintings of Madonna, of Jesus, of saints is much desired. Also anything old from Europe. Ras Rillstein say you are merchant with many connections. I have money arranged in London and need to fill boat very soon."

Grotius looks at him searchingly and then, apparently satisfied, says, "I will provide you with names of suitable traders. If you have money ready immediately, they will be pleased to deal with you." He glances at Forlan.

"And if you wish, Mr. Khalid, go you to the drinking house, called 'the Corner House', opposite the cross at Charing Cross in The Strand. Forlan will guide you. Look at the items on the wall. There are also paintings. If you like any, tell me and we shall do business."

"I am deeply grateful," says Khalid.

Edward's Notes. Part 5

So now I knew that the Gabriella had gone to Abyssinia.

She had started in Italy, went to France, then to England and now to Abyssinia. I had been lucky to be able to track her from Bellini's workshop, to an auction in Paris, to a will and then to a business account in England, and onwards to Abyssinia. From 1470 to 1790.

But now I reckoned I had probably small chance of finding her again as Abyssinia most likely didn't keep the kind of records that would help me. I was encouraged, though, because Abyssinia was a Christian country where Mary was regarded as the Queen of Heaven and various saints were worshipped with the utmost devotion. My only chance was to read the journals and writings of travellers to Abyssinia in case they mentioned any European paintings there. Unlikely, but I had to give it a go. There were many travellers and I read them all. You know the kind of thing; 'Travels by Mule in the Dark Continent', 'Where Men and the Desert Meet'.

A tedious task. Well, actually, not that bad, because you can quickly see if there's going to be anything useful by flipping through the pages. Anyway, there was no mention of Gabriella. In fact there were no mentions of any paintings in Abyssinia other than their own, perhaps not surprisingly.

Then I came across a Mrs. Cornelia Speedy and her travel writings. Her travel book, 'My Wanderings in the Sudan' was very well received, apparently. She travelled about North West Africa and the Middle East with an india-rubber bath and her husband Charlie.

Captain Charles Tristram Speedy was actually a well-known explorer, adventurer and army officer. A big fellow, 6 foot 6 inches tall, red-haired and 'built like Hercules.'

Before they married, Captain Speedy had played an important part in the British government's expedition to Abyssinia of 1868. This expedition was sent to rescue the British Consul who had been imprisoned by the Abyssinian Emperor Theodorus. The Emperor considered himself insulted because a letter he sent to Queen Victoria had not been answered.

Captain Speedy never wrote anything about Abyssinia, although he gave a speech to a girls' school in London which was written up by one of the girls present.

"A certain Captain Speedy has just returned from Abyssinia and gave us an amusing talk about it. He won our gratitude when he ended by saying, 'I understand that you girls have to write an account of my talk to you. Well, the very word Abyssinia means confusion, because the races are confused, the *religion is confused, the mountains and valleys are confused and I know that I am confused in addressing so many girls. So the more confused your accounts are, the better they will represent the country and the lecture."*

He was also a bit of a poet and wrote some lines for his intended, Cornelia, entitled, 'The Inventory of a Captain's Room': (This is 1868, remember, florid stuff with medieval influences):

'A large battered sofa, four feet at the head,

By day made a couch, by night is a bed,

A mould to cast bullets, a couple of flutes,

The bowl of a pipe and an old pair of boots.

Three swords and one scabbard, a box of cigars,

Some Lundy Foote's snuff and Brown Windsor in bars,

A letter from home and a library book,

An old hat and a powder-horn hung on a hook.

A fine cambric glove, a lock of dark hair,

Both highly prized gifts of some lady fair.'

He was much written up in the press when the Abyssinian Expedition was over and the consul rescued from the fortress of Magdala, Theodorus' stronghold. 'The Graphic', a popular newspaper of the time, noted that 'the name of no Englishman is more connected with the recent history of Abyssinia than that of Captain Speedy.'

And it was in that fortress that the Gabriella portrait hung on a wall in the throne room and where it was acquired by Captain Speedy, at the end of the campaign. The merchant Khalid had sold it to a warrior chief and the son of this chieftain fought his way up to become Emperor of Abyssinia. He cherished the portrait, apparently, because it reminded him of his beloved first wife who died young.

A large British army, with a contingent of 46 elephants no less, trekked four hundred miles up country to the fortress of Magdala to besiege Theodorus and his fanatically brave troops.

Captain Speedy was welcomed on the expedition by the Commanding Officer, General Napier, for a number of reasons.

How the expedition came about was very interesting.

EXT. PICCADILLY, LONDON - DAY

People going about their business stop to buy 'The Times' from a PAPER BOY.

> PAPER BOY
> Read all abaht it! British consul thrown in dungeon! Not seen for weeks! 'orrible death expected!

Public read avidly. Discuss in shocked tones.

> A VOICE
> We should send in the troops!

INT. NAVAL AND MILITARY CLUB, PICCADILLY - DAY

A group of gentlemen in leather club-chairs read 'The Times'.

> SENIOR MEMBER
> Good God! A British Consul

imprisoned by a damned upstart
calling himself an emperor!

                    SECOND MEMBER
The poor fellow's been there weeks!

                    SENIOR MEMBER
Confound it! A person holding the
position of Consul is considered by
all governments, civilised and not
civilised, as sacred!

                    SECOND MEMBER
Quite so. Something must be done!

Leaning against a gilded fireplace behind them
is CAPTAIN CHARLES SPEEDY, early 30s, 6'6",
broad, muscular.

                    SPEEDY
Not easy.

                    SENIOR MEMBER
What?

                    SPEEDY
Abyssinia is a damned difficult
place to get to and this emperor's
palace - actually a fortress - is a
long way up-country

SENIOR MEMBER
Well? Are you suggesting we do
nothing? Let the poor fellow rot?
Damn fine thing that would be!

SECOND MEMBER
Surely we could send in a cavalry
contingent - a flying column -
speed and surprise you know. Might
do the trick.

SPEEDY
Magdala is four hundred miles from
the coast. Through some of the
roughest terrain I've ever seen.
Deserts, ravines, mountain ranges,
rocks as big as villas, and every
kind of weather from ice storms to
110 in the shade. Hostile tribes
at every turn.

He sips his whisky and soda, reflectively

SENIOR MEMBER
Harrumph!

SPEEDY
What is more, the Emperor likes
nothing more than to fight. He
brutally conquered all the other
war-lords of his country, and those

he didn't kill he threw in his dungeons. No-one would be happier than he, if we send a rescue expedition.

EXT. OUTSIDE MAGDALA - DAY

Theodorus parades his warriors. He sits on throne in an open area.

Line after line of warriors gallop at full tilt towards him.

 Some wheel away at full speed; others come to a sliding halt before him.

Muskets are fired in the air and spears are thrown at moving targets, some of which are prisoners, running for their lives.

Theodorus is delighted, and laughs and drinks with his chiefs.

Flambaud, his adviser, keeps his glass filled.

EXT. OUTSIDE PARLIAMENT, LONDON - DAY

Large numbers of the public parade up and down, holding banners reading 'RESCUE OUR CONSUL', 'SEND TROOPS NOW' and SHOUTING slogans.

INT. DISRAELI'S OFFICE IN PARLIAMENT -
SAME TIME

Prime Minister DISRAELI and Foreign Secretary
LORD STANLEY look out the window of a book-
lined room, listen to the shouting outside.
Both are in their 50s; Stanley, elegant and
distinguished; Disraeli, dressed in a dandyish
manner, his hair in ringlets. Disraeli closes the
window.

                    DISRAELI
          There's no other way of looking at
          it - something has to be done. The
          people are angry, the Army is
          impatient, and when I saw her
          yesterday, Her Majesty looked very
          grave.

                    LORD STANLEY
          Indeed!

                    DISRAELI
          There are two matters at issue. Can
          we do it and at what cost?

                    LORD STANLEY
          Of course, nothing is beyond our

capabilities. But the cost is high.
The Secretary of State for War has
made the calculation. 7 millions.

DISRAELI
7 millions!

LORD STANLEY
A very large amount, by anyone's
reckoning. He has based it on the
premise that we must do everything
necessary to avoid a second Crimea.
I am entirely of his opinion. We
must never have another breakdown
of our military system like we had
at Sebastopol.

DISRAELI
Of course not. But 7 millions. To
save the life of one...

LORD STANLEY
...British Consul.   The person of
an envoy is sacred.

DISRAELI
Quite. It is also a question of the
prestige of England. Of her
reputation and honour.

                    LORD STANLEY
          We are left with no choice. But
          the House may not like it.

                     DISRAELI
          I will take care of the House.

He opens the window - the SHOUTS of the
crowds are heard.

               How did this unfortunate - this
               most unfortunate - predicament come
               about?

          THREE MONTHS EARLIER

INT. FOREIGN OFFICE, LONDON - DAY

An elderly MESSENGER walks through a series
of elegant rooms where assistant under-
secretaries, officials, clerks are busy working at
desks, taking down files from shelves, writing
memoranda, dictating to secretaries.

There is the BUZZ of business in hand,
conducted in a stately manner. This is the hub
of Empire.

The messenger stops outside a double door,
knocks and enters.

INT. OFFICE OF SENIOR OFFICIALS - SAME
TIME

A sumptuously furnished room with a huge
map of the world covering almost the whole of
one wall. Many countries are coloured pink.

A double sided desk is piled with official
papers. On either side of the desk two
officials, HARRY and HAMMOND review the
day's correspondence.

The messenger hands a document - all seals
and ribbons - to Harry.

> MESSENGER
> Just arrived, sir. By frigate from
> Aden.

> HARRY
> Thank you, Jones.

> HAMMOND
> That looks interesting, Harry.
> What is it?

Harry opens the document carefully.

> Well, let's see. Hm. Addressed to
> Her Majesty? It appears to be a

letter from a chap calling
himself.... the 'Emperor of Abyssinia'!

HAMMOND
Really? From Abyssinia, eh? In
Africa, somewhere, I believe.

Harry goes to wall map and pulls down a more
detailed chart.

HARRY
Yes, there. Between Egypt and the
Sudan.

HAMMOND
Ah ha! See that, Harry? It's just
across the water from Aden! Not our
bailiwick, Harry.

He rings a small silver bell on his desk. A
CLERK enters immediately.

CLERK
Sir?

HAMMOND
Take this round to the India Office,
immediately, please. Hand it
personally to Mr. Murray with the
compliments of the Foreign Office.

INT. INDIA OFFICE, LONDON - DAY

The clerk walks through a majolica ornamented courtyard, up an immense staircase lined with statuary and into another series of elegant rooms full of people working, some in foreign dress. Here, the buzz is more pronounced.

The clerk knocks on another set of double doors and enters.

INT. SENIOR OFFICIALS' OFFICE - SAME TIME.

An office furnished with heavy mahogony furniture and large case clocks. MURRAY and MERIVALE work at separate desks.

The clerk hands the letter to Murray and exits.

>   MURRAY
>   And what is the Foreign Office
>   sending us this time, I wonder?
>   More confusion, no doubt. Let me
>   see. Ah! Addressed To Her Majesty.
>   Hm. From the... Emperor of
>   Abyssinia. The Emperor of
>   Abyssinia? Who on earth is he
>   and - more to the point - what does
>   he want? Hm. Hm. Hm. I'll be

damned! Wants us to help him fight
the Turks and kill off his unco-
operative relatives! And what's
this? There's some very odd
phrasing here, Merivale. Good God!
He seems to be proposing marriage!

The clerk re-enters.

> CLERK
> Excuse me, sir Ways and Means
> Committee.

> MURRAY
> I must be off, Merivale.

He hands the letter to Merivale.

> File and forget. Unquestionably.

> MERIVALE
> Of course.

He writes on the side of the letter: "Mr. Murray
says
nothing to be done on this".

INT. ANTE-ROOM, MAGDALA - NIGHT

A room lined with shields and spears.

Theodorus is drinking heavily. Flambaud ensures his glass is never empty.

> THEODORUS
>
> I wrote to this Queen Victoria. I have asked from her a sign of friendship. But it is refused to me. She sends no reply! None! Does she think her ancestors are more illustrious than mine? I, who have made a bargain with God. God has promised not to descend to earth and strike me; and I have promised not to ascend to heaven and fight with him! Ha! And yet this woman Queen! This woman Queen. She....She... Where is her reply?

> FLAMBAUD
>
> Consul Cameron should have brought it, Sire.

> THEODORUS
>
> Yes! Consul Cameron...I don't trust him. He is too proud for an underling. Come.

INT. CAMERON'S CELL, MAGDALA - NIGHT

Cameron, flanked by two guards, stands before

Theodorus.
Flambaud stays in the doorway.

>   THEODORUS
> Consul Cameron. Consul Cameron.
> WHERE IS YOUR QUEEN'S REPLY! Eh?
> Is she so proud she cannot reply to
> me? On your knees, Consul!

Cameron is pushed to the floor by the guards.

>   THEODORUS
> Flambaud! Come here. Do you know
> who lies here?
>
>   (He kicks Cameron viciously.)
>
> This is - Queen Victoria!

INT. HOUSE OF COMMONS, PARLIAMENT - DAY

A packed house, MEMBERS OF PARLIAMENT
lounging on their benches.

Disraeli is at the rostrum, in mid-speech. An
accomplished orator.

>   DISRAELI
>
>   ....and the time has arrived
>   when it is necessary for Her

Majesty's government to take action...

He looks around the chamber.

...to vindicate the honour of the
Crown and to protect Her Majesty's
Consul from further harm.

'Hear, Hear' from the benches.

Her Majesty's government are of the
opinion that any rescue expedition
should be organised in India. In
preparation for laying forth this
matter to the House, My Hon.
Friend the Secretary of State for
India, telegraphed to the Governor
of Bombay for information concerning
the disposition of Indian troops
and steamers for transport and the
organisation of a competent
commissariat.

Nods of approval from the benches.

Furthermore, it was proposed that
General Sir Robert Napier - by
common consent one of our ablest
Indian officers - be asked to
provide recommendations for a
rescue expedition. This he has done.

General Napier suggests a force of 40,000 men, of which 12,000 of the front line. Less than this, he avers, would leave the expedition with over-extended lines of communication, rendering it vulnerable to the enemy.

I now wish to speak of the probable cost. We believe the amount, which is on the whole the wisest and best to consider, is 2 million pounds.

Lord Stanley stares at him briefly.

This estimate refers to expenditure in a distant country and therefore must be described as a 'rough'estimate. Although I call it a 'rough' estimate, it is not a 'careless' estimate.

He looks up again, very gravely, as though daring his listeners to speak.

By no means. It has been submitted to as severe an examination as possible.

Lord Stanley is studying his fingernails.

If we are called upon to re-inforce
the army, then the estimate might
become 3 million 800 thousand. In
round numbers, then, 4 millions.

Some members look puzzled.

I submit it is a small sum of
expenditure in such a cause. We are
not going to war to obtain
territory. We are not going to war
to secure commercial advantage. No
gentlemen.

He thrusts out his chest, places hand on hip,
holds his chin
high.

We go to war for a high moral cause.
We do so to protect the prestige,
the reputation and the honour of
England! When the standard of St.
George is raised on the mountains
of Abyssinia, this petty tyrant
will know what it means to twist
the tale of the British Lion!

The puzzled frowns disappear, replaced by
cheers.

In the Public Gallery, reporters scramble to

leave.

EXT. OUTSIDE PARLIAMENT - DAY

Crowds mill about excitedly. Gentlemen shake hands.

Hats are thrown in the air, cockneys dance, children run about shouting 'bang'.

Officers look proud and eager.

THE BRITISH LINES AT ASHANGI CAMP, ABYSSINIA.

INT. GENERAL NAPIER'S TENT - NIGHT

Selected officers and war correspondents sit around a long table, heavy with crystal glass, silver cruets, candlebra and the remains of a dinner, being cleared away by the General's Indian servants.

The muffled sounds of the camp permeate the walls of the tent. COMMANDS, MARCHING FEET, camels and mules BRAYING, the CRY of 'Post. All's well!'.

Decanters are passed to the left as diners

replenish their glasses.   Jovial conversation, occasional moderated LAUGHTER; bonhomie prevails.

General Napier presides, flanked by the Adjutant.

> GENERAL NAPIER
> Captain Speedy. Welcome. We hope to benefit from your advice; from your Abyssinian experiences.

> SPEEDY
> Thank you, sir. I am at your disposal.

> GENERAL NAPIER
> I am sure all of us would be interested in your views on Theodorus. You were once his military adviser, I believe.

> SPEEDY
> In a manner of speaking, sir. I drilled his troops for a while and I was one of his favourites. But I retreated to New Zealand when I heard of a plot by rival officers to tip me over a cliff.

Laughter from around the table.

GENERAL NAPIER
You were a favourite?

SPEEDY
Yes, sir. Largely because I could
slice a cooked sheep in half with
one strike of my sword. Um,
lengthways.

Exclamations and more laughter.

GENERAL NAPIER
H'm. And Theodorus himself?

SPEEDY
He is an excellent shot and a fine
horseman. Most of his life has been
spent fighting rebellious tribes,
so he has much experience of
campaigning. His warriors are also
excellent horsemen. They are, of
course, armed only with spears and
muskets. However, he is a firm
believer in the use of cannon and
even has his own foundry at Debra
Tabor.

GENERAL NAPIER
Does he, by Jove! I read
somewhere that, when younger,
Theodorus was an enlightened

ruler - in his way.

SPEEDY

Yes, he was. He abolished slavery
and barbaric penalties for crimes,
prevented soldiers from plundering
villages, and tried to keep the
peace between the constantly
warring tribes.

I don't wish to introduce sentiment
to this table, sir, but, with your
permission, I think it's relevant.
He had a wife whom he adored -
Tewabeh. She was a very sweet girl
and she was able to bring out his
best qualities. I once made a small
drawing of her, which she put in a
gold locket for him to wear. I
never saw him without it. She died
two years after their marriage. He
was inconsolable. Devastated, in
fact, and her death quite changed
him. A damned sad affair. Now, he
has become extremely cruel and
uncontrollable. In his drunken
rages he is capable of any atrocity.

GENERAL NAPIER

And is there not a troublesome
adviser?

SPEEDY
Indeed. One Flambaud. An
extraordinary fellow. He used to
be a gun-runner down here. A nasty
piece of work, sir, and one who has
a malign influence over Theodorus.

GENERAL NAPIER
We must talk more en route, Speedy.
Now, gentlemen, if we are to leave
tomorrow at first light, we should
perhaps retire.

WAR CORRESPONDENT
Excuse me, sir. May I ask a question?

ADJUTANT
          (sotto to the General)
Henry Morton Stanley, sir. Of the
'New York Herald'. Much travelled
in Africa, I believe.

GENERAL NAPIER
Please do, Mr. Stanley.

STANLEY
Well, General. You have amassed a
large force of soldiers. With a
great deal of armaments and stores.
And Abyssinia is the sole surviving

country in Africa not yet
colonised. Is it the intention of
Her Majesty's government to add
Abyssinia to the British Empire?

GENERAL NAPIER
No, it is not, sir! Our task is to
rescue the Consul. Nothing more. I
will tell you clearly what are my
intentions. We shall proceed to
Magdala and rescue Consul Cameron.
No peacable inhabitant of this
country will be molested. All non-
combatants and their property shall
be protected. All supplies
required for my soldiers shall be
paid for. There is no intention to
occupy any portion of Abyssinia.

STANLEY
With respect, General, it's still a
big force to rescue one individual.

GENERAL NAPIER
I will tell you why, Mr. Stanley.
During the war in the Crimea, our
soldiers died more from bad
organisation and disease than from
the enemy's bullets. Here, in
traversing Abyssinia, we shall meet
some of the most difficult country

to be encountered anywhere. We must
feed and maintain our soldiers over
400 miles of mountainous terrain
and hostile tribes. Nonetheless, I
have every intention of bringing
this expedition to a successful
conclusion. To do that, I judge it
necessary to have the resouces you
see about you.

Nods of agreement round the table.

Well, gentlemen. The Punjab
Pioneers have prepared a way for us
tomorrow. Shall we withdraw?

ADJUTANT
Excuse me. Sir.

GENERAL NAPIER
Yes, what is it?

ADJUTANT
Sarn't Major of the Scinde, sir.
With a captive.

GENERAL NAPIER
Advance, Sar'nt Major.

SAR'NT MAJOR enters, a magnificent
moustachioed figure, with two men and a

struggling, limping Abyssinian warrior.

> SAR'NT MAJOR
> Sarn't Major Singh, sir. We
> captured this fellow. His horse
> ran lame and we caught him, sir.
> Hold still, you savage!

> GENERAL NAPIER
> Where is he from? Was he trying to
> steal our rockets?

> SARN'T MAJOR
> He won't answer to a single
> question, sir. Not at all.

> GENERAL NAPIER
> Well, I want to know why he is a
> hostile in a territory where we
> have negotiated safe passage.

> WARRIOR
> Hey! No safe passage in Abyssinia
> for English!

> GENERAL NAPIER
> Ah! It speaks.

> WARRIOR
> Is our country - not yours! Hey!

>   Theodorus will drive you out! He
>   will sweep down upon you! He is
>   cunning as fox. He sees like lynx.
>   He is braver than lion! Beware of him!

The staff, amused, admire his bravura.

>   WARRIOR
>   Theodorus! He never shuts his eyes.
>   He will meet you! He will strike you!

His expression changes from anger to joy.

He struggles free and leaps forward to Speedy.

>   WARRIOR
>   Fellecca! Hey! Fellecca!

>   SPEEDY
>   Welda!

They embrace, stand back, regard each other
affectionately.

>   GENERAL NAPIER
>   I presume you two are old friends?

>   SPEEDY
>   Indeed we are, sir. This is Welda.
>   A brave and resourceful warrior.
>   To whom I taught the few phrases of

English you have just heard.
Unfortunately, totally loyal to
Theodorus.

GENERAL NAPIER
As he has so abundantly made clear.

SPEEDY
He'd best go to the medical tent.
Come, Welda. General Napier doesn't
want your blood on his floor. With
your permission, sir.

GENERAL NAPIER
I suppose he won't enlist with us.

WELDA
Hey!

GENERAL NAPIER
No. Quite.

Edward's Final Note.

So I thought I'd look a little deeper into the Speedy family and found a posting on the web from a descendent out in Australia who had come across some old letters and diaries belonging to Mrs. Speedy. Heaven knows how they found their way to Australia because Captain and Mrs. Speedy spent most of their lives in India and Malaysia. This descendent was putting them up on the web for family relations with a hankering for famous ancestors. In one of the pages from Mrs. Speedy's diary of 1869 there was a reference as follows:

"Charlie had a most distressing experience on his way back to England from Magdala. He had decided to travel through Europe and see some of the cultural sights, before taking up his next post in India.

He stopped off for a few days in Prague and put his portmanteau in the store room of the

Hotel Wenceslas. When he went to get it, it had disappeared. Charlie is an impressive being when he's angry, but I'm afraid it was to no avail. The portmanteau was never seen again.

When Magdala was finally taken, there was as usual much looting by the British troops, the intention being that the looted items would be sold off and the proceeds shared out among the troops. Charlie bought some daggers and two European oil paintings which, surprisingly, had been in Theodorus' chambers, and a few other gimcracks, all of which he had put in the missing portmanteau.

One of the paintings was a portrait of a girl which seemed quite old and he was looking forward to finding out who painted it. It didn't have a signature but in the corner there was a 'Z' painted. He was so angry it had been stolen from his luggage."

Well, there we are. Gabriella is presumably still in Prague, as I've checked that no records have come up concerning her sale or auctioning off. I'm going to ask Boulton to have a good scout around over there. We know that the locals are selling up their paintings to make a few pennies - as you'll see, we sell them on over here - but we haven't come across any major artist's work, yet.

It's a damned nuisance I've got this far and may not live to see the famous portrait after all.... Well, that's the way it is.

Of course, I may be completely off track, made too many assumptions, got too obsessed about the search, and, who knows, the painting may no longer exist. Still, I can't believe that my intuition might have let me down....

I'm feeling bloody awful now so I think I'll sign off for a bit.

I do hope you will carry on the search and be successful.

My love to you, Ben, and God Speed. Say hello to Gabriella for me.

The Trip to Liberech.

We fly to Prague and take a taxi to the city. The taxi driver says nothing the whole journey and concentrates on chicaning through the other traffic.   Spread out on the shelf above the dash are soap, a few small toys, a mobile phone and a deodorant stick.   Hanging from above the windscreen are good luck charms and his I.D. card which gives his blood group and says his name is Vaclav Pechar.   He swerves into the parking space in front of the Babylon Hotel on Wencesplatz and hits the brakes hard.

   "Good!" he says.   Our bags, computers and document cases are picked up by a youth with dyed red hair who disconcertingly vanishes as I pay Vaclav.

   "Good!" he says again, shakes my hand enthusiastically and gives me his card.   It's in Czech of course, which I can't read, so I hand it to Dobri. We push our way through a noisy group of German teenagers and go in what appears to be the collonaded main entrance of the hotel.   But it's not. It's the entrance to a large and busy coffee-room in which two ancient gentlemen are playing violin and piano, in full evening dress.

"Table for two, sir?" asks a waiter.

"No thanks," I say, "Hotel?"

"Next door." So we try again.   At reception, a letter is waiting for us.   It's from Boulton's contact Mr. Slama and reads:

'Welcome to Praha.   Please to meet at Casino Red Dog at 13.30 hours.   Thank you.   Yours faithfully.   K. Slama.'

The youth with the red hair and our bags appears and shows us to our rooms.   On the way up he says:

"Manchester United, very good." I give him a big tip.

"See you in the bar in five minutes," says Dobri.

My bedroom is large, has creaking floors and a brand new bathroom, in which hangs a sign saying:

'Please regret water shutdown. Water return 19.30 hours. Thank your understanding.'

In the bar, which is a circular balcony overlooking the ancient gentlemen playing the violin and piano, we have time for only one quick Bellini. We agree that Dobri will take a background role and not mention his Czech origins in our meeting with Mr. Slama.

At the Casino Red Dog, the doorman looks at us with a welcoming leer. I say "Mr. Slama, please." He sniffs and gets a boy to show us upstairs. We pass through a huge and noisy, smoke-filled room where the gaming tables are crowded with Czechs and tourists, mostly Germans it seems. Mr. Slama is sitting in a red plush booth peering into his brief case. He jumps up and pumps our hands.

"Welcome. Welcome to Prague. Good trip?"

"Yes, thank you," we say.

"Three becherovkas," he says to the boy.

"So, here you are. Prague very beautiful city. Many beautiful girls. Ha, ha. But we do business.

"Absolutely," I say.

K. Slama is stocky, has a sallow complexion, bad teeth, wears black clothes and a large Rolex. He has an ancient mobile phone I don't recognise and a carton of two hundred cigarettes, half empty.   He smokes continuously.

"You represent big gallery?"

"We do," I say. " In the West End of London."

"H'm," he responds, looking a little suspicious.   After a short pause, he thrusts a menu at us and says:

"Something to eat?   A light little lunch?"

Nothing on the menu looks light, so I decide to eat hearty and choose a 'Mydlar Axman's Chop', which turns out to be leg of pork, while Dobri orders "Garlic Soup, Timber Men's Style."   Mr. Slama orders an omelette.

"Stomach fragile," he says, lighting another cigarette.   "So. Your gallery interested in very special paintings, yes?"

I nod my head.

"I have many," Slama continues.

"Good. Who is actually the owner of these paintings?"

"Don't worry. We meet principal. Tonight," he adds proudly.

"Tonight?"

"Yes. We drive to Hotel Jested in Liberech. Is not far. You have car?"

"No."

"O.K. We hire." He opens his mobile, which has two scuffed US flags printed on it, and mutters into it.

"Is done. You pay later with euros, please."

For our journey to the Hotel Jested, Mr. Slama suggests that one of us should drive while he navigates. I offer to drive. The car is a large old Tatra and is comfortable in an American way with wide seats and a fierce heater. Mr. Slama takes 100 euros from me, hands 80 to the car-boy and then pockets the other twenty. After one hour of driving, he says,

"Not far, now. Left here, please."

We turn onto a single track road and start climbing interminably up a hillside into wreaths of evening mist. We pass a ski lift and I negotiate several difficult bends and rocks in the road. This is not easy as the Tatra's steering seriously lacks precision and I think something is loose underneath. At the top of the hill is the Hotel Jested.   It looks like an elongated rocket, round at the base, with its nose lost in the mist. The car park is on the edge of what appears to be a cliff so I park with great care. There are no other cars visible between the boulders.

Mr. Slama leads us into the restaurant which is empty except for one table at the back, at which sits a large man with a low forehead. On the table are four glasses and a bottle of vodka. He heaves himself up and greets us. Mr. Slama says,

"Mr. Kakonin.   Mr. Fletcher and Mr. Denn from London."

 Mr. Kakonin grunts and sits down. His heavy features and small eyes are obviously not used to smiling a lot.

"Wodka," he says, pushing two glasses towards us, which he fills to the brim. Slama helps himself. I raise my glass to them.

"Good Luck."

"Hah!" shouts Kakonin and we drink.

"You interested my pictures, yes?" We both nod.

"What for?"

"What for?" I ask.

"What you do with them?"

"That depends on many things," I say.

"What things?"

"First we must clean them to see what they might be. If they are of no importance artistically, then too bad. If they look like they might be old then we must restore them. A long and expensive business. A big risk. If they restore well, then we must establish who painted them. That would decide their value. Then we sell them."

"What kind of profit, you make?"

"That depends entirely on the current market value of the painting. Is the artist fashionable? Are there potential clients who are interested in that particular artist? And so on."

"My paintings worth 100,000 euros. Very good paintings. All old. One is signed with letter

'L'." I tap Dobri's heel.

"Is Leonardo da Vinci, probably," says Kakonin.

"Every one of Leonardo's paintings is accounted for,' says Dobri. 'Only his drawings are not fully catalogued. Is it a drawing?"

He turns and bellows, "Karenina!" A young woman enters the restaurant behind him. She is wearing white thigh-length boots, a black and very short plastic mini-skirt and matching tank top. Her blonde hair is cropped and she has a face tattoo of three small gold stars and she carries three old paintings in gilded frames. Kakonin looks at them and shouts at her again. She turns round and struts out returning immediately with a fourth painting, which he grabs from her.

He lays it on the table before us. "Is Leonardo!" Dobri and I lean forward.

"It's not a drawing," I say. "And it's extremely dirty." But I can see it is a portrait of a girl. And the 'L' is sloping.

"And the others," I say. He passes them over one by one. They vary in size although none is big. One is of St. George and the Dragon, one is a Virgin and Child, one is a coastal view and

188

one is so dirty it is impossible to see what it portrays. I turn to Dobri.

"What do you think?"

Dobri picks up each one and turns them over. He points at the torn backcloths, the rotting frames. He turns them over again and peers at the pictures.

"Very poor condition, unfortunately."

"OK," says Kakonin. "If you not interested I have other buyers waiting. Please do not waste my time." He turns to Slama.

"When do Americans come?" He looks at us.

"I have Americans very interested." He pours himself more vodka.

"Americans?" I say. "Well, Mr. Kakonin. I can tell you frankly that Americans are not keen to buy material they cannot see. These pictures would not appeal to them. Too dirty. Too much of a risk. Especially at your price of 100,000 euros."

"Maybe so. Final question. Are you interested or not."

"May I ask where these pictures came from?"

"Have been in my family for generations." I

notice Slama is studying his vodka intently.

"You want to buy or not?" asks Kakonin.

"Yes," I say. "In principle." I turn to Dobri.

"Can these be restored to good condition?"

"Not all of them."

I pick up the 'St.George and the Dragon' picture.

"This one is a possible. Art lovers like this stuff with the dragon," I say, ad libbing, "And the coastal scene - if that is what it is - is a possible, also. The 'Virgin and Child' is not very saleable whoever painted it. This one is too dirty to know what it is. And the one with the 'L' appears to be a portrait. Again not easily saleable. Who wants a portrait of someone if it's not connected with their family? Still, I suppose we could take the risk. The whole lot would seem to be worth about 30,000 euros and that is what we would be ready to pay."

"You are stupid! These pictures are valuable!"

"I don't think you will get a better offer elsewhere, but if you want to try...."

Kakonin slaps the table, stacks up the pictures and indicates to Slama to get up. They walk towards the door. Dobri looks pale. I reach for the vodka bottle with one hand and cross fingers with the other. I must get in with my next offer before they go through the door. But Kakonin stops and turns.

"50,000!"

"Mr. Kakonin, "I say. "I can offer no more than 40,000. But that 40,000 is here in Liberech. In cash. We can exchange now." Kakonin and Slama return to the table.

"Exchange now?" he asks. "You take pictures and you give the money. 40,000?"

"Yes."

"Where is the money?"

"All we need to do is that both of us sign this piece of paper which is a sales document and then I will give you the money."

We do the deal and Kakonin disappears into the back of the hotel.

The fog is now very thick and I back the car slowly away from the cliff edge. I can't see anything behind.

  "I can't see anything behind," says Dobri. The rear of the Tatra hits a rock. I drive slowly forward and eventually find the way out.

"Is Corbusier prize-winner," says Slama.

"What?"

"Hotel Jested."

This guy Slama is too much, Kakonin is too much and the vodka was also too much, but at least we have the picture.   I open the window to get some fresh fog. When we finally get back to Prague, we drop Slama off at the Casino Red Dog and pull up outside the Three Violins Cafe.

The Three Violins Cafe is a single large room with a vaulted ceiling. A notice in an elaborate gilt frame hangs on the wall and reads:

'Already in the 16th.century this famous building belonged to the Court Painter of Emperor Rudolf II, and violins were made here.   It became later the most important violence workshop in Prague.'

Dobri and I sit at a long table and order coffee and buns and review the situation. The painting is placed carefully on the table between us. I ask him how he will go about authenticating it.

"There've been a lot of ways of identifying painters' work - there was even a school which said look at the ear. Many artists paint the ear the same way no matter what the subject's ear actually looked like. Or the shape of the hand. Then there's simple connoisseurship. You know, the biggest expert on the artist looks at the picture and then gives his opinion. But for me, digital imaging is the best by far. A multi-spectrum camera can show you the layers of pigment, the weave of the canvas, and the way the brush strokes are applied. These can then be compared with the same images from a fully authenticated painting. It's foolproof. So that's what I'll be doing when we get it back to London. After I've cleaned it. Very gently."

"Dobri," I say. "Would you mind taking the picture back yourself? I have something I want to do here and I need to stay on a few days."

Epilogue.

If you're sitting in the Alta Praha restaurant in Prague, that is, if you're sitting in the big semi-circular window, then you have an all-embracing view of the river Vltava and the old town with its multi-coloured roofs, old church steeples and huge castle. If you fancy eating the chef's signature Czech dishes then you order pâté of duck liver and smoked duck breast, cream espuma with foie gras, marinated white radish, and espuma of cranberries and red currant, as a starter, followed by baked drake breast, red cabbage confit with apples, warm red wine jelly, and boiled potato dumpling. Chilled Ryzlink Rýnský - late harvest, Habánské Sklepy 2008/09 is a good accompaniment. You finish up with strawberry mousse on strawberry powder with home-made macaron, much admired by the locals.

The young couple sitting at table 5 have ordered these dishes, although the girl had been tempted to have the pastry pocket of coconut ice cream, strawberries and mango sauce. Maybe next time. Their heads are close together when they are not eating and they smile at each other a lot and they seem very happy. He frequently places his hand on hers.

"We'll have to leave for the airport, soon," he is saying.

"I know," she replies. "But we will come back to Prague from time to time, won't we?"

"Of course."

The young man looks quite well in his dark suit. He has an amiable face and a confident manner. But the girl, she is a beauty. Truly lovely. Auburn hair piled high on her head, a slender neck with tendrils curling onto it, a heart shaped face, dark eyes under arching brows, a mouth which almost pouts, a feminine and gentle manner....

The young man's mobile buzzes. He groans. "Excuse me," he says, raising his eyes to heaven, and looks at the screen. It is a text message from Dobri, 'Pls call asap.'

"I have to call Dobri," he says. "Won't be long, I promise." He strides off to the foyer.

A waiter appears and clears the dishes, smiling at her. When he has gone she puts her elbow on the table, rests her chin in her hand, and looks out at the town.

In a corner of the foyer, the young man calls the London number. When he returns the girl is sitting looking pensively but happily at the rooftops. She is so beautiful, he thinks, still marveling that she should be with him.

"The painting is genuine," he says. "The real thing! A Bellini portrait of the girl Gabriella."

He signals to a waiter. "Please ask the bartender if he can do two Bellini cocktails."

THE END

Other books by John Problem:

The Bankers' Assassin
A thriller

The Government's Top Salesman Tells All
A political satire/comedy – selling off Britain

The Fearless Four and The Messenger
The Fearless kids have lost their parents

Seven Short Stories for Dogs

For more information please visit:
http://tiny.cc/y9twjw

Printed in Great Britain
by Amazon.co.uk, Ltd.,
Marston Gate.